# CLAWS!

# GOOSEBUMPS HorrorLand™
## Also Available from Scholastic Audio Books

# GOOSEBUMPS HorrorLand™
## HALL OF HORRORS

# CLAWS!

## R.L. STINE

SCHOLASTIC INC.
New York  Toronto  London  Auckland
Sydney  Mexico City  New Delhi  Hong Kong

ISBN: 978-0-545-28933-7

Goosebumps book series created by Parachute Press, Inc.
Copyright © 2011 by Scholastic Inc.

12  11  10  9  8  7  6  5              11  12  13  14  15  16/0

Printed in the U.S.A.                                        40
First printing, March 2011

# WELCOME TO THE
# HALL OF HORRORS

## THERE'S ALWAYS ROOM FOR ONE MORE SCREAM

You're right — you can't find it on the HorrorLand map. This old castle is a place for very special visitors only. This is a place for kids who have stories to tell.

Step inside. Welcome to the Unliving Room. Yes, it's cold in here — cold as the grave.

Come sit by the fire. I like the way the flames make the shadows dance on the wall. Want to hear something strange? When the fire is out, the shadows *still* dance on the wall.

I am the Story-Keeper. Here in the darkest, most hidden part of the park, I keep the doors to the Hall of Horrors open.

Kids find their way here. Frightened kids. Haunted kids. They are eager to tell me their stories. I am the Listener. And I am the Keeper of their tales.

Those shadowy faces on the wall? They are paintings of the kids who brought their

1

frightening tales to me. Funny how their eyes seem to follow you around the room—isn't it?

We have a visitor today. That boy sitting by the fireplace, so pale, with his hands clasped so tensely. His name is Mickey Coe.

Mickey is twelve. A nice-looking young man. But something has creeped him out. Let's go talk to him.

"What is your story about, Mickey?"

"It's about a black cat."

"Aah, yes. A black cat. You may not know this, but black cats can be *lucky*."

"Not for me," Mickey says.

"Well, go ahead, Mickey. I am the Story-Keeper. Start at the beginning. Tell me your story."

Mickey swallows. He makes a gulping sound. "Are you sure? It's pretty weird and scary," he says.

Go ahead, Mickey. Don't be afraid. There's Always Room for One More Scream at the HALL OF HORRORS. . . .

"Let me hold her for a while."

Amanda grabbed the cat from my hands and bumped me out of the way. She bumped me so hard, I almost fell onto the couch.

"You don't have to grab," I muttered.

"It's faster, Mickey," she said. "You're as slow as a banana."

*Banana?*

She's *weird.*

The Caplans laughed. "I thought you were best friends," Mrs. Caplan said. "Do you always argue like that?"

"No. Never," I said.

"Yes. Always," Amanda said.

Mrs. Caplan is a tall woman with long, straight black hair, thick black eyebrows, and big green eyes. She loves to wear bright colors, red and purple and yellow.

She has a deep voice and speaks as if she's

onstage. She told us she wanted to be a Broadway actress. But she ended up a drama teacher in the high school instead.

Mr. Caplan is shorter and less colorful. And quiet. He has short, wavy hair, mostly gray. And he wears round, black-framed glasses that make him look a little like an owl.

He was our fifth-grade teacher last year. He was a pretty good teacher, except he talked about his vegetable garden too much.

And it was kind of weird having your next-door neighbor for your teacher.

Bella, the Caplans' black cat, settled into Amanda's arms and purred softly. Amanda grinned at me.

I knew what that grin was saying. *Bella likes me better than you, Mickey.*

"Bella doesn't usually like to be held," Mr. Caplan said, scratching his gray hair.

"She's a sweet, sweet cat," Mrs. Caplan said. "But she's not a lap cat."

"She sure has taken to you, Amanda," Mr. Caplan said.

Amanda flashed me that obnoxious grin again.

She should be nice to me. *I'm* the one who got us this cat-sitting job.

But no problem. I'm used to my friend Amanda Underwood.

4

I mean, she has lived across the street from me my whole life. So she's like a tree ... or a rock ... or a mailbox. You know. Something that's just always been there.

Amanda seems a lot sweeter than she is. She is about two inches shorter than me. She's kind of tiny and looks about nine or ten, even though she's my age, twelve.

She has straight copper-colored hair, big blue eyes, and a tiny mouth shaped just like a little heart.

A *lot* of words come from that tiny mouth. I mean, she says about a hundred words to my one. And she talks really fast, like she's always excited and in a big hurry.

I guess I'm the quiet type — especially next to Amanda.

Don't get me wrong. Amanda and I are best friends. We really like each other.

We just don't always get along.

"So let me get it straight," Amanda said, gently petting Bella's back. The cat had her eyes closed and made soft purring sounds. "We come here to your house twice a day and feed Bella and give her water."

Mr. Caplan nodded. "That's right. And clean the litter box. Don't forget that part."

"That will be Mickey's job," Amanda said.

Nice!

"We'll be sailing for six days," Mrs. Caplan said. She moved her arms to show ocean waves. "But you can reach us if you need to. I'll leave you the numbers."

"I'll leave you my brother's number, too," Mr. Caplan added. "In case you have any trouble."

"We can handle it. Easy job," I said.

"We won't have any trouble," Amanda said. "Look how sweet Bella is."

The cat raised her head and gazed up at Amanda with her bright yellow eyes.

"She is so awesomely sweet," Amanda said, cuddling the black cat.

Famous last words?

You have no idea.

The horror didn't start until the second afternoon.

The idea was to care for Bella twice a day — before school and after school. It was an easy job. And fun — especially for me because I've always liked cats.

And the Caplans were paying us each fifty dollars for the week. Not too shabby, right?

The first day was good. We went in the morning before school. Bella seemed glad to see us. She meowed and rubbed against our legs.

"She's hungry," Amanda said. "I'll feed her while you scoop out the litter box."

"And tomorrow we'll trade jobs?" I asked.

"Why would we do that?" Amanda replied.

It was early in the morning. I didn't feel like fighting with her.

We fed Bella and petted her a little. Then we locked the door carefully behind us and hurried to school.

That afternoon, Amanda let me feed the cat. Bella gets dry food in the morning and wet food in the afternoon.

I had a little trouble opening the can. The pull-top snapped off.

"You're as clumsy as an onion," Amanda said. I told you she was weird. "Use the electric can opener, Mickey. Want me to do it?"

"I can handle it," I said.

I opened the can easily. Pulled off the lid. Forked the disgusting, fishy stuff into Bella's bowl.

"Don't give it to her like that," Amanda said, grabbing the bowl from me. "You have to mash it up first."

"Since when are *you* the cat expert?" I asked.

"Since today," she answered.

Bella sat on her haunches, staring up at the food bowl. Her yellow eyes didn't blink.

I don't think she cared if the food was mashed up or not. But Amanda always thinks she knows everything.

Bella gulped the food down hungrily.

"Should we play with her or something?" I said. "Think she's lonely?"

Bella answered the question for us. She licked the bowl clean. Then she ran off to another room.

"Maybe cats don't get bored or lonely," I said.

"You have something disgusting stuck in your nose," Amanda said. "I've been meaning to tell you all day."

"All *day*?" I cried. "You waited *all day*?"

She tossed back her head and laughed.

"Mickey, how is it going with Bella?" Dad asked me at dinner that night.

"Perfect," I said.

"If you have any trouble, just ask your mom or me for help," he said.

"Okay," I said. "But there won't be any trouble."

Wrong.

The next morning, we fed Bella and gave her fresh water. Amanda picked her up and put her in her lap. The cat pawed at her. She tapped Amanda's shoulder like she was trying to tell her something.

That made Amanda laugh.

Then I heard her mutter, "Uh-oh. Oh, noooo."

"What's wrong?" I asked.

Amanda was tugging hard at Bella's tail. "We have a little problem," she said.

# 3

"Problem?" I hurried over to them on the couch.

"My bubble gum," Amanda said, tugging at the black fur on Bella's tail. "It flew out when I laughed. And now it's stuck to her tail."

I bent down and studied the pink blob stuck in the black fur.

"Why were you chewing bubble gum at seven-thirty in the morning?" I asked.

"I always have bubble gum after breakfast," Amanda said. "It helps get the egg taste from my mouth."

She gave a hard tug.

The cat yowled and tried to jump away.

"Help me hold her!" Amanda shouted.

I grabbed Bella around the middle. She swiped at me with her front paws and tried to squirm out of my hands.

"Can't you twist the gum off?" I asked, struggling to hold the cat still.

"Her fur is all stuck to it," Amanda said. "I have to cut it off."

She pushed Bella at me. I gripped her and held her tight against my chest. The cat's heart was beating so hard.

I tried to calm her down. But her back was stiff and she held her tail straight out.

Amanda ran to the kitchen. A few seconds later, she returned carrying a pair of scissors. "Hold her still," she ordered.

"I'm trying," I said. "She doesn't like this."

"She's being very good," Amanda said. "She's a very good cat."

Amanda slid one hand down the cat's tail. I couldn't bear to watch. "Just don't cut her tail off," I said.

*Snip snip.*

"All done," Amanda said. She held up a glob of pink gum covered in fur.

Bella pulled free and jumped to the floor. She turned and stared at us, her tail curling up behind her.

"Amanda, look what you did!" I cried. "She has a bald spot on her tail." There was a circle bigger than a quarter where I could see the pink skin poking through.

Amanda shrugged. "It'll probably grow back before the Caplans get home," she said. "Cat fur grows fast."

I shook my head. I felt kind of shaky.

11

Bella lowered her tail and padded into the other room.

"You can't even see the bald spot," Amanda said. "No one will notice."

"We're going to be late for school," I muttered.

Amanda laughed. "Look at you, Mickey. You're white as a sheet and you're sweating!"

"So?"

"So what would you do if we had a *real* emergency with the cat?" Amanda asked.

"Totally freak out?" I joked.

We both laughed.

After school, we went to my house to drop off our backpacks. In my room, my goldfish were staring out of the tank at me. I picked up a box of fish food and started to sprinkle some into the water.

"Not like that." Amanda grabbed the food box from my hand. "Just give them a little at a time, Mickey. You don't want fat goldfish — do you?"

"Huh? Fat goldfish?" I tugged her hair just to be annoying. "Are you the goldfish expert, too?"

She ignored me and moved to the cage where I keep Zorro, my white mouse. Zorro twitched his pink nose and poked it through the cage bars. He likes attention.

"Are you sure he's getting enough exercise?" Amanda asked.

"Why don't you go on *Animal Planet*?" I said. "You could be the expert on every animal."

Amanda tickled Zorro's head. "Maybe I will," she said. "Are you giving him carrots and fresh fruit?"

"What's up with all the advice?" I said. "*You're* the one who stuck bubble gum to Bella's tail."

"Accidents happen," Amanda said. Laughing, she shoved me out of the way so she could be the first one down the stairs.

We crossed the driveway, bumping each other, trying to knock each other over. And we were still arguing about who was an animal expert and who wasn't.

When we were inside the Caplans' house, it took a while to find Bella. She was in the laundry room, pressed between the washer and the dryer. It was a cozy spot. Maybe she stayed there a lot. Or maybe she was playing hide-and-seek with us.

She stared up at us with those yellow eyes. Stared hard. Of course, we knew what she wanted—her dinner.

Amanda and I turned and started for the kitchen. Bella stood up and followed us.

We were crossing the front hall when I saw something that made me gasp. "Oh, no! The front door!" I cried.

We had left it wide open.

I started toward it but bumped into Amanda. It took me a few seconds to catch my balance.

"Noooo!" I shouted as Bella took off, running toward the open door.

"Bella! No! Bella—stop!" Amanda and I screamed.

But the cat lowered her head and kept running.

"Bella—wait! Bella!"

The cat flew out the open door and darted down the front lawn.

We chased after her. My heart pounded so hard, my chest hurt. Amanda came right behind me, screaming Bella's name.

I stopped short when I saw the big red truck rolling down the block.

Bella ran into the street.

My scream rose over the squeal of the brakes.

The truck skidded hard.

I heard a horrible high screech.

I saw the truck tire bump over Bella.

The truck jolted to a stop.

Then . . . silence.

The driver's door swung open. The driver jumped down and came running toward us.

He was a big man with scraggly black hair and a short black beard. His belly bounced under the shirt of his wrinkled blue uniform.

"Bella! Bella?" Amanda had her hands cupped around her mouth and was still shouting the cat's name.

But we both knew the truth.

"I'm real sorry!" the truck driver called as he raced to the sidewalk. "I—I couldn't stop in time."

"I don't believe it," Amanda said in a whisper. She covered her face with her hands. "This didn't happen. No way."

The driver stopped a few feet in front of us, breathing hard. "The cat—it ran right under my tires," he said. "I'm real sorry. There was nothing I could do. It happened so fast."

I tried to answer him, but the words caught in my throat. I was shaking so hard, I grabbed on to Amanda's shoulder to keep from falling over.

Her whole body trembled. She had her hands over her face. She kept repeating, "This didn't happen. It didn't. It didn't happen."

I felt sick. Like I was going to puke. I kept swallowing, trying to force it down.

"I really tried to stop," the truck driver said softly. He bowed his head. "Sorry. I'm real sorry."

He turned and walked slowly back to his truck, keeping his head lowered.

A few seconds later, he started the truck engine and rumbled off.

"The C-Caplans," I stammered. "What are we going to say to them?"

Amanda finally lowered her hands. Her cheeks were wet from tears. She shook her head. "I don't know, Mickey. How can we *face* them? We killed their cat."

"It—it was an accident," I started. "We—"

"No, it wasn't," Amanda said in a whisper. "We were arguing and we didn't realize. We left the door wide open. It's our fault. It wasn't an accident."

Her shoulders shook.

My stomach churned. A groan escaped my throat.

"The body," Amanda whispered.

I stared at her. "What did you say?"

"We have to get Bella's body," Amanda said. "We can't just leave her in the middle of the street like—like roadkill."

*Roadkill* . . . The words repeated in my mind. *Bella . . . roadkill.*

If only I could push a REWIND button. Make time go back just a few minutes. Just long enough to close that front door and save Bella's life.

"Okay," I said. I took a deep breath. I started walking slowly to the street.

"Wait up, Mickey," Amanda said. Her voice trembled. "We'll go together."

My legs were shaking as I stepped onto the curb. "We need a trash bag or something," I said.

"No, we don't," Amanda replied. "Look." She pointed to the street.

I squinted up and down. I gasped in shock.

"Bella's body—it's *gone.*"

# 5

We stood together staring down at the street. The late afternoon sun was lowering behind the trees. I felt a cool breeze that made me shiver.

"I think the truck driver took the body," Amanda said finally.

I nodded. "Yeah. He probably didn't want us to see her squashed flat."

I checked the grass on the other side of the street. And squinted down the curb again. No sign of Bella's body.

I suddenly had the feeling I was about to cry. *No way* I wanted to do that in front of Amanda. I turned my head away, and the feeling slowly faded.

I still felt sick. My stomach was churning, and I had a heavy feeling in my chest, as if I'd swallowed a rock.

Amanda and I started walking toward my house. We didn't say anything till we reached the front door.

"My parents will be home soon," I said. "We have to tell them what happened. Right away."

Amanda nodded. "I guess." Her voice cracked on the words.

I pulled out my phone. "Maybe I should call my mom," I said. "Before she gets home."

"Why?" Amanda asked.

I shrugged. "Guess I just feel like telling someone. I know it won't make anything better. But . . ."

I flipped open my phone.

"Wait." Amanda grabbed my arm.

The phone fell out of my hand and bounced on the concrete stoop. "Hey — why'd you do that?" I cried. I picked up the phone. It was okay.

"I have an idea," Amanda said. Her blue eyes flashed. I could see she was thinking hard.

I took a step away from her. "What kind of idea?" I asked.

"Maybe I'm brilliant," she said. "Maybe."

"What kind of idea?" I repeated. "I don't like the look on your face. Whenever you get that look —"

"Mickey, shut up and listen to me," she said. "There are a million black cats in the world, right?"

I stared at her. I didn't answer.

"Well, what if we go to a pet store or the pound or something? And we find a black cat that looks like Bella."

My mouth dropped open. "I c-can't believe you're thinking this," I stammered.

"We find another black cat," Amanda continued. "And we substitute it. We bring it to the Caplans' house. And when they come home, we act like it's Bella. Like nothing bad ever happened."

I stared at her. I couldn't speak.

"It could work," she said softly.

"Amanda, it's crazy," I said. "It's totally insane."

"Let's try it," she said.

I tried to stop her. I had a hundred questions. But she had an answer for all of them.

"What makes you think we can find a cat that looks just like Bella?"

"Mickey, we won't know unless we look."

"What if it has a completely different personality?"

"Cats are cats."

"Let's say we get a new cat. And the Caplans come home and see right away it's not Bella. What do we tell them?"

"Let's worry about that when the time comes," Amanda said.

I couldn't win. I couldn't stop her.

She sat down in front of my laptop and started to search.

It was hard for me to sit still. I had to keep pacing back and forth. It was like my legs had a life of their own.

I kept hearing the scrape of the truck tires, the squeal of the brakes. Again and again, I saw that big truck skidding into the little cat.

The cat Amanda and I were responsible for.

And now Amanda had this crazy plan that I knew would only get us into deeper trouble.

She leaned over the keyboard and typed quickly. The glow of the screen made her face look bluish green. Like she had turned into some kind of monster.

*Calm down, Mickey.*

My thoughts were getting out of control. If only I could shut my eyes and make the whole day disappear.

"Here it is!" Amanda cried. "Perfect. Come over here and check this out."

I sighed and stepped up behind her. I leaned forward to study the screen.

"It's a store called Cat Heaven," Amanda said. "See the map? I know how to get there."

"What makes you think they have black cats?" I said.

She scrolled down. "Look."

I saw row after row of photographs. Cats of every color and size. Lots of black cats, too.

"These are all for sale?" I said.

Amanda nodded. "Stop wasting time. Let's go." She jumped up and pushed me out of the way. "Do you have your bus pass?"

I glanced at my SpongeBob wall clock. Almost five. Mom and Dad would be home soon.

"Wait one second," I said. I scribbled a note to my parents. I told them I was working on a project with Amanda. I wasn't lying—right? I said I'd be home in time for dinner.

A few minutes later, we were on the North Central bus on our way to Cat Heaven. I stared out the window and tried not to think about poor Bella. I tried to force her horrifying last screech from my mind.

I didn't even realize I had pressed my hands over my ears to shut out the sound.

Amanda pulled my hands down. "Mickey, what's wrong?" she asked.

"Nothing," I said.

And then I opened my mouth in a scream as a HUGE yellow-eyed cat—its mouth open, fangs bared—rose up in the bus window.

"Mickey—stop!" Amanda cried. "You've got to calm down. It's just a sign."

"Huh?" I was breathing hard. "Sign?"

Amanda pointed. "It's a big billboard for Cat Heaven." She laughed. "You didn't really think it was a giant cat—did you?"

"Of course not," I said. I could feel my face turning hot. I knew I was blushing.

We climbed off the bus at the next stop. The sky was gray. The sun had disappeared behind the trees. The cool breeze felt good against my hot cheeks.

Another giant billboard showed a grinning orange cartoon cat. Amanda and I crossed the wide asphalt parking lot heading to the store. I saw only four or five cars parked in the lot.

The store towered over us, all glass and dark metal. CAT HEAVEN. A blue neon sign—at least two stories high—blinked on and off above the glass entrance doors.

"Wow," I muttered. "This place is enormous."

"It's as big as a Walmart." Amanda agreed with me for once. "And all they sell is cats."

"Well . . . maybe they *will* have a Bella look-alike," I said.

Amanda slapped me hard on the back. "Good attitude," she said, smiling. "Keep it up, Tomato Brain."

*Tomato Brain?*

The glass doors slid open and we stepped into the store. I blinked, waiting for my eyes to adjust to the bright light.

A strange odor greeted us. It was sweet but lemony. Like air freshener. I guessed they pumped it through the store to cover the cat smell. It definitely didn't smell like a pet store.

We took a few steps into the store, still blinking and trying to focus. I saw row after row of wire cat cages. The aisles seemed to stretch for miles.

The walls were covered with huge posters of cats. The cats in the posters were all grinning. And they were all resting on puffy white clouds — like they were in heaven. Each cat had a gold halo floating over its head.

Soft, tinkly music played. I could barely hear it over the meows and yowls of the caged cats. The cat cries were deafening.

I suddenly remembered being on a camping trip deep in the woods with my parents. And

25

crickets started to chirp all at once. Thousands of crickets all around us. All chirping and chirping until you couldn't hear yourself think.

The cats in this store were even louder than that.

All down the aisles, I could see them pacing in their cages. Prowling. Pawing the cage walls. Trying to set themselves free.

"This is way weird," I muttered to Amanda. "It—it's like a horror movie."

She pushed me away. "No, it isn't," she said. "It's just cats in cages. How scary is that?"

I didn't answer. I didn't want her to think I was a total wimp. And I didn't want to argue with her.

What I really wanted was to *get out* of this store and go home.

I didn't know why they called it Cat Heaven. The cats didn't seem happy at all. They all seemed restless and totally stressed out.

"Let's start at the first aisle," Amanda said.

The first aisle was far in the distance. I saw that the aisles were numbered with white signs. We were standing at Aisle 38.

We were halfway to Aisle 1 when a smiling young woman in a gray uniform hurried up to us. She had short, curly blond hair, dark eyes, and a sparkly diamond stud on one side of her nose.

The name tag on her uniform shirt was shaped

like a cat. It read: LUCY. She gave us a friendly wave with one hand. I was surprised to see she was wearing gloves.

"Hi," she said. "Welcome to Cat Heaven. Can I help you?"

"Why are you wearing gloves?" I blurted out.

Her smile grew wider. "Sometimes they bite," she said.

"Is there a special black cat section?" Amanda asked.

Lucy shook her head. "No. They are all mixed in everywhere," she said. "We tried to organize the cats once. But we couldn't do it. Just too many cats. And more come in every day."

"Do you have a lot of black cats?" I asked.

"A lot," Lucy replied. "Like maybe a hundred or two?"

"Awesome," Amanda said. "Could we just look around?"

"No problem," Lucy replied. She handed Amanda a red plastic figure of a cat with a button in the middle. "Push the button if you find a cat you like," she said. "It's a beeper. Push it and I'll be able to come find you." She giggled. "Don't get lost. If you get stranded somewhere deep in the aisles, it could be weeks before anyone finds you. You'll have to live on cat food."

Nice thought.

Lucy walked away chuckling about her little joke.

27

I gazed down a long row of cats prowling and pawing and clawing at their cages. Some batted at little balls that were hanging from the cage roofs. Others slept, curled up tightly.

"Aisle one?" Amanda said.

"Aisle one," I said. We had to shout over the cat yowls.

Our shoes tapped the brown linoleum floor as we trotted to the far wall. The first cage in Aisle 1 held two sleek cats, tan with dark fur on their faces. One of them slept. The other one stared out at us with narrow, slitted eyes.

A sign under the cage door read: SIAMESE, scrawled in black marker.

We started down the aisle, walking side by side. We peered into each cage.

No black cats in Aisle 1. Amanda and I reached the back wall of the store. It was mirrored, which made the rows of cages look even longer than they were.

We started down Aisle 2. We were about halfway down this aisle when a man's voice rang out: "Hey, you two. Here is the cat you're looking for!"

**8**

A tall store clerk in a gray uniform stood several cages down from us. As we walked closer, I saw that he had slicked-back black hair, a long nose that jutted down from two tiny, round black eyes, and a pointed chin. He looked like he was half bird or something.

He smiled at us. His smile was crooked. It made his mouth tilt up on one side. "I've got the one you're looking for," he repeated. His voice was hoarse and high.

He pointed into a cage at an orange-and-white cat. The cat sat on its haunches, calmly watching us, its tail wrapped under it.

Amanda and I both let out sighs of disappointment.

Did we think the man was a mind reader?

The cat-shaped tag on his shirt read: LOU.

"Sorry," Amanda said. "That's not the cat we're looking for."

Lou blinked his little bird eyes. "This guy is

on special today. You can name your price. Take him for a dollar. Look what a sweetheart he is. Best cat in the store."

"I don't think so," I said. "We're looking—"

"I'll give him to you for free," Lou said. "Here." He started to open the cage door. "Totally free if you buy a twenty-pound bag of cat food."

"No thanks," I said. "We—"

"Too old? You're looking for a kitten?" Lou asked.

"No. We're looking for a black cat," Amanda said.

"Oh. A little bit of good luck, huh? Most people don't know that black cats are lucky."

"Not too lucky today," I muttered. Again, I heard the squeal of brakes in my head.

Lou's phone rang. He pulled it from his pocket and flipped it to his ear. He waved us away. "Go browse. Browse," he said. "Catch you later." He started to talk into his phone.

We hurried away from him. He wasn't going to be of any help.

We stopped at a cage halfway down the aisle. There it was—our first black cat! It was batting a ball around and didn't look out at us.

"Too big," Amanda said.

We trotted down the long row. At the very end—another black cat. This one was the right size.

"Wrong color eyes," Amanda said.

We moved on.

The next black cat was also about Bella's size. And it had yellow eyes.

"Its fur is a little shaggier than Bella's," I said.

"No. The fur is okay," Amanda said, bringing her face right up to the cat's cage. "But look."

It took me a while to figure out the problem. The cat had no tail. Just a short stump on its back end.

I groaned. "Are you sure you want to keep going?"

"Of course," Amanda said, trotting on ahead of me. "We just started, Clam Face."

"But don't you see how crazy this is?" I demanded.

She ignored my question. I had no choice but to catch up to her.

We explored row after row. We looked at maybe thirty black cats. None of them matched Bella.

There was always something wrong with them. Too tall. Too fat. Eyes not the same. Teeth different. Paws too big. Too young. Too old. Face just didn't match.

Finally, I lost it.

We were at the back wall, somewhere around Aisle 20. I was standing in front of a wooden door with large red letters stenciled on the front: KEEP OUT.

"ENOUGH!" I screamed.

Amanda spun around to stare at me.

"Enough! I want to get out of here!" I yelled. I balled my hands into tight fists.

"Mickey—" Amanda motioned with both hands for me to cool down.

"This isn't going to work!" I cried. "We're not going to find a match, Amanda. This is totally insane. You're crazy! CRAZY!"

Okay. I admit it. I already said I lost it.

But the cats were driving me crazy. Hundreds of cats meowing and yowling and pawing and clawing.

"Don't call me crazy, Prune Head!" Amanda screamed back at me. I think she lost it, too.

She shot out both arms and gave me a hard shove in the chest.

I was used to being shoved around by her. But this was harder than usual.

I stumbled back—into the door marked KEEP OUT.

I hit the door, and it swung open. I fell into a back room. I felt myself swallowed in darkness. A deep darkness, silent and cold.

I fell onto my butt, blinking, my heart pounding.

"Hey—" I choked out. "Where am I? What *is* this room?"

Amanda poked her head into the room. "Mickey? Are you okay?"

I climbed to my feet. I brushed off the seat of my jeans. "Yeah. Fine," I said. "Do you think you could stop pushing me all the time?"

She shrugged. "Maybe."

She pulled the door open wider and stepped into the room. "*Brrr.*" She hugged herself. "Why do they keep it so cold back here?"

"I think it's a storage room," I said. I turned around. And realized I was wrong.

"Oh, wow."

I was staring at more rows of cages. The cages were sitting on long tables. Were there cats in these cages? I squinted into the darkness, struggling to see.

Yes. There were dark figures in the cages. Dark and still.

"More cats!" I told Amanda.

"But they're silent," Amanda said.

I gazed around. The room had a high ceiling, gray plaster walls, no signs or posters of cats with halos.

Gray evening light washed down on us from a row of small windows up near the ceiling. Dust floated in the beams of light. The air smelled sour.

I squinted into the nearest cages. Cats shifted from side to side silently. They stared back at me with dull eyes.

Amanda took a few steps along the nearest table. She leaned forward, trying to see the cats clearly in the dim light.

I shivered. I realized the room was so cold, I could see my breath.

"Let's get out of here," I said. "Come on. I—I don't think these cats are for sale."

Amanda didn't answer. I saw her halfway down the aisle. She had stopped. She wasn't moving.

"Amanda?" I called. "Hey—we're not supposed to be back here. Come on—let's get going."

She didn't move.

"What's your problem?" I called, my voice suddenly high and shrill. "Amanda? Hey—Amanda? What's wrong?"

# 10

I had a fluttery feeling in my chest. Suddenly frightened, I forced myself to move.

I trotted down the row of cages toward Amanda. My shoes kicked up dust.

I grabbed her arm. "Amanda? What's up with you? Didn't you hear me calling you?"

She stared into the cage in front of us. Her mouth hung open. Her eyes were wide.

I turned and followed her gaze. I stared at the black cat lying in the cage. The cat stared back at us with dull yellow eyes.

"It—it looks a lot like Bella," I choked out.

Amanda nodded. She finally found her voice. "A lot," she whispered.

I lowered my face until it was just an inch or two from the wire cage.

The cat didn't move. For a moment, I thought maybe it was stuffed. But then it blinked and shifted its tail behind it.

"It's the same size as Bella," I said. "Is it a female?"

"Think so," Amanda murmured. "Look, Mickey. It has the same yellow eyes. And kind of the same face, don't you think?"

I studied the cat. Yes. Yes. The fur was the same length as Bella's. I couldn't see the cat's face clearly in the dim light. But it seemed pretty much the same.

The cat yawned. It made a soft whining sound as it did.

"I think I saw Bella yawn like that once," Amanda said. She squeezed my shoulder. "Mickey, I think this is the cat we want. I think we've found the right cat. Yaaay!"

I realized my heart was pounding. I was excited, too. Could this crazy idea of Amanda's actually work?

The cat stood up suddenly. It made a small circle, its tail curling around its body.

"It's a female," Amanda said. "She is almost perfect, don't you think?"

I couldn't stop a grin from spreading across my face. "Yes!" I pumped a fist in the air. Then I bumped knuckles with Amanda. "I think this is definitely Bella Two," I said.

"We'll bring her to her new home and let her get acquainted with it," Amanda said. She had her eyes on the cat as it circled its cage.

"The Caplans won't be home for four or five

days," I said. "That will give Bella Two plenty of time to make herself at home and get used to everything in their house."

"When they get back, they won't notice a thing," Amanda said. "Am I a genius? Or am I a genius?"

"Don't get crazy," I said. "You're not up to genius yet. First, let's buy Bella Two and get her home. Push the button on that buzzer. It'll call that girl Lucy."

Amanda pulled the buzzer thing out of her pocket. I reached for the cage latch and started to swing open the wire door.

And an angry voice from the doorway boomed: "Step back from that cage. What are you two *doing* back here?"

**11**

I closed the cage door and jumped back. I bumped into Amanda and we slammed into the table behind us.

The man came running toward us, his footsteps heavy on the concrete floor. As he came nearer, I recognized him. The tall sales guy we met up front—the one named Lou.

Breathing hard, he swept back his oily black hair. "You can't—" he started.

But Amanda interrupted him. "We'd like to buy this cat," she said. She patted the side of the cage.

"No. Sorry," Lou replied. "You shouldn't be back here. It's off-limits to customers."

"But we found the cat we want," Amanda insisted.

Lou shook his head. "Sorry, guys. These cats are special. They're not for sale."

"Special?" I said. "How do you mean, special?"

Lou gazed at me, but he didn't answer my question. He motioned to the door. "We need to get you out of here," he said.

Amanda put on her best pleading face. She made her eyes really wide and her mouth all pouty. "But we really really *really* need this cat," she said.

"We'll pay double," I said. I don't know where that idea came from. It just popped out of my mouth.

"Yes," Amanda quickly agreed. "We'll pay double for this one. Whatever it costs. And we'll be your best best friends for life!"

That made Lou chuckle. His tiny eyes flashed for a second.

"Trust me, guys," he said, shaking his head. "I don't think you want that cat."

"But—but—" we both protested.

"Come up front with me," Lou said. "I have plenty of black cats you will like." He turned away from us and started to the door.

Amanda leaned close and whispered to me: "We need this cat. Not another black cat. What are we going to do?"

Lou was waiting for us in the doorway.

Suddenly, I had an idea.

"We'll go up front with him," I whispered to Amanda. "Distract him somehow. Make a fuss or something. Just keep his attention. You're good at that."

"And what are *you* going to do?" Amanda demanded.

I pointed to a back door. It was narrow and made of solid wood, nearly hidden in darkness at the far wall.

"You keep him busy," I whispered. "I'll sneak back in here. I'll grab the cat and run out through that back door."

Amanda gasped. "You mean *steal* her?"

I stared over Amanda's shoulder at the cat. The perfect cat.

"We have to," I said. "We don't have a choice."

Amanda had a strange look on her face as we followed Lou out of the back room. I knew I had surprised her. She is usually the bold one.

We walked down a long aisle of cages toward the front of the store. We stopped in front of a cage. Lou pulled out a black cat. He held it in his arms for a moment. Then he started to hand it to Amanda.

But Amanda tossed back her head and let out a loud sneeze.

She sneezed again. Again, even louder and harder.

"I think I'm allergic to this cat."

She went into a total sneezing fit.

Perfect. What an actress!

Time for me to move. Lou had his eyes on Amanda. I took a deep breath and crept as fast as I could down the aisle to the back room.

My heart pounding, I reached for Bella Two's cage door. I fumbled with the latch. Swung the door open.

I reached inside for the cat.

Would she give me a hard time? Try to squirm away?

No. She just stood there and let me wrap my hands around her middle.

Carefully, slowly, I lifted her out of the cage.

She seemed very relaxed. She didn't tense up her muscles at all. She didn't paw at me. And she didn't make a sound.

*What a sweet, gentle cat,* I thought.

I could hear Amanda sneezing her head off in the front of the store. Lou was calling for someone to help her.

I lifted Bella Two onto my shoulder, and I strode quickly to the narrow back door. I held her tightly against me with one hand. I could feel her heart beating steadily on my shoulder.

I gripped the door handle with my free hand — and pushed.

The door didn't budge.

I looked for some kind of lock. No.

I pushed again. The door was jammed.

I switched the cat to my other side. Then

I lowered my shoulder—and smashed it into the door.

Pain shot down my arm, down my side.

But the door didn't budge.

I glanced all along the back wall. No other doors.

I was stuck. No way out.

# 12

The cat lowered her head against me and clung to my shoulder.

I gazed all around for an escape route. Panic made my blood pulse at my temples. I was breathing rapidly, short, wheezing breaths.

I heard a whistle. Like a police whistle.

"Huh?" I raised my eyes to the open door.

I saw Lou running toward me. He had his eyes on the cat in my arms.

Amanda stood behind him, her eyes wide with fright. "Run, Mickey!" she shouted. "Run! He—"

Her voice was cut off by another loud blast of Lou's whistle.

A clanging alarm went off. Cats began to yowl.

"Stop right there! Drop that cat!" Lou screamed over the noise.

He blew his whistle again as he came thundering up the aisle toward me.

I gripped the cat tightly. I froze for a moment, froze in total panic.

Then I started back to the door. In my panic, I bumped into a row of cages. I sent them tumbling to the floor.

The cages clattered loudly on the concrete. Doors flew open. Cats came slithering out.

I didn't care. I had to get Bella Two out of there.

I lowered my shoulder and barreled into the narrow back door.

One last try. One last desperate try.

I went crashing into the door—*and it swung open.*

"Yesss!"

I stumbled out of the store. I nearly dropped the cat.

Pressing her to my shoulder, I caught my balance and started to run. I could still hear the clanging alarm and Lou's angry shouts behind me.

My shoes thudded in the empty parking lot. Cats wailed and cried. Did other cats escape?

I could see the street curving up ahead at the end of a wide patch of tall weeds. Huge trees at the edge of the road cast long black shadows over the weeds.

The sun had gone down. The sky was charcoal gray. The cool wind brushed my hot face.

I swung back, gasping for breath. The back door of the store stood open. But I didn't see Lou or any store clerks coming after me.

The black cat stretched her paws over my shoulder and lowered her head. She didn't try to squirm or pull away. I couldn't believe how calm she was.

The wind sent a Coke can rolling across the pavement. I nearly tripped over it. A sharp pain stabbed my side as I ran as fast as I could. I wanted to reach the trees, where I could hide.

"It's okay, kitty. It's okay," I murmured as I stepped into the tall weeds. They shifted from side to side in the night breeze. They brushed the legs of my jeans as I ran to the trees.

I ducked behind a wide tree trunk and waited. I sucked in breath after breath. I knew the tree hid me from the store. Pressing my back against the tree, I listened for Lou's shouts and his whistle.

Cars moved slowly along the crowded street. People were still driving home from work. Headlights swept over me.

Holding the cat tightly, I dropped to my knees behind the tree. I needed to catch my breath. I needed to try to think clearly.

But I let out a scream of surprise when a voice right behind me shouted:

"Where's the cat?"

# 13

I spun around. "Amanda!" I cried. "I—I didn't see you!"

She hunched down in the weeds. She pointed at Bella Two on my shoulder. "Is she okay?"

"Yeah. Fine," I said. I stared behind her. "That store guy—?"

"I didn't see him," she said. "I ran out the front and circled back."

She lifted the cat away from me and held her in her arms. "How are you doing, Bella?" she asked, speaking softly. She rubbed the cat's back. "Yes, your name is Bella now."

The cat purred.

"Calm as a pineapple," Amanda said.

"Well, *I'm* not," I said. "We killed one cat. Now we've *stolen* another one. We have to get home, Amanda. We—"

"Look how sweet and gentle she is," Amanda said. "She's perfect, Mickey. I think our luck is changing."

Just as she said that, I heard Lou's shouts from the parking lot.

I raised my head over the weeds. I saw Lou running hard, waving both arms wildly. "Stop! You two! Stop right there! STOP!" he screamed.

Amanda and I jumped up. We turned and ran. The weeds rustled and bent as we pushed through them to the street.

Glancing back, I saw Lou, still waving and shouting. He reached the edge of the parking lot. He dove into the weeds, coming after us. "Stop! Stop! Both of you!"

Amanda and I had no place to run. We stood on the edge of the road. Cars honked at us as they rolled past.

"He's got us trapped!" I cried. "We can't escape him."

Amanda held on to Bella tightly. I watched Lou thrashing his way through the weeds. He was only a few yards away from us.

When the bus pulled to a stop, I cried out in surprise. *"No way!"* I didn't realize we were standing at a bus stop.

Amanda and I dove onto the bus.

The driver squinted at Bella. "Pretty cat," he said.

The bus doors slid shut just as Lou came bursting out of the weeds.

The bus pulled away. I saw the angry look on Lou's face. He shook both fists in the air. I couldn't hear him, but I could see he was still shouting furiously.

Amanda and I stumbled to the back of the bus. We sank down in the backseat. We were both still breathing hard. My face was drenched in cold sweat.

We didn't speak all the way back to the Caplans' house. Bella was totally calm, as if nothing special was going on.

We were carrying her up the Caplans' driveway when my phone rang. I pulled it out of my pocket. "I know, Mom," I said. "Sorry I'm so late. Amanda and I got hung up with the cat. I'll be home in five minutes."

I didn't lie — right? We really did get hung up with the cat.

Now I began to worry about how this new cat would act being in a strange house. She had been perfectly calm so far. But being in a new place with strange rooms and strange smells . . . would it freak the cat out?

Would she smell the old Bella? Would that make her upset?

Only one way to find out.

We carried Bella Two into the Caplans' living room. This time, I carefully closed the front door. Amanda set the cat down gently on the rug.

The cat just stood there for a long moment. She gazed up at Amanda. But she didn't look around. And she didn't seem eager to go exploring.

She waved her tail slowly from side to side. Then she took off suddenly. Her paws padded the carpet silently as she darted around the couch, onto the tattered pillow beside it on the floor.

Amanda and I exchanged glances. "That's the old Bella's favorite spot," I said. "And the new Bella went right to it. Weird."

"Weird as a raspberry," Amanda said.

*Raspberry?* Before I could try to figure that one out, Bella leaped up from the pillow. She ran into the kitchen and stopped at the space beside the fridge.

She lowered her head and licked her empty food dish. Then she meowed, like she was asking for her dinner.

I turned to Amanda. "How did the cat know where her food dish was?" I asked.

Amanda shook her head. "Beats me. She ran right to it."

"Maybe she smelled it," I said.

I pulled a can of cat food out of the cabinet. I opened it, then forked it into the food dish.

The new Bella dug in to it, chomping and slurping as if she hadn't been fed in days. She made the funniest noises, gulping and coughing as she sucked down the fishy-smelling gunk.

"Wow, she was *starving*!" Amanda declared. "Don't they feed the cats in Cat Heaven?"

Hearing the name of the store made me shudder. I pictured stealing the cat again. And our narrow escape. I pictured Lou, all red-faced and furious, shaking his fists at us as we roared away on the bus.

I knew I'd have nightmares that night.

Bella licked her food dish till it was sparkling clean. Then she lapped up some water from the water bowl.

Amanda had a big grin on her face. "Look at her, Mickey," she said. "Look how perfect this cat is."

I had to agree. She looked a lot like the old Bella. She was about the same size. Her yellow eyes were the same. Her tail was just about the right length.

"She even has the same cute perked-up ears," I said. "This could work, Amanda. It really could. Maybe you *are* a genius!"

Her grin grew wider. "Told you so."

I started to bump knuckles with Amanda. But before I could reach her, I saw the cat sway back onto her hind legs.

Bella pulled back her lips, bared her teeth — and let out a shrill screech from deep inside her. Her eyes started to glow bright yellow.

Before I could move, she leaped off the floor. Leaped high into the air.

"Whooooa!" A shocked cry burst from my throat as the cat landed on my chest. I staggered back.

She screeched again. It sounded like a scream in a horror movie.

Her eyes glowed brighter. I saw her teeth . . . saw her claws poke out from the furry paws.

No time to move. No time to push her away.

The cat swiped her claws down my chest— and slashed the front of my T-shirt in two.

# 14

*"Owwww!"* I let out a howl of pain.

The cat dropped to the floor, landing on all fours. She took off running and disappeared down the hall.

I staggered back against the fridge. I pulled apart my slashed T-shirt and examined my chest.

"Did she cut you?" Amanda demanded. "Are you bleeding?"

"N-no," I stammered. My voice came out in a choked whisper. "I'm only scratched. She didn't break the skin."

Amanda shook her head. "I don't believe it. She ripped your shirt to *rags*."

"What was *that* about?" I said, trying to pull the two sides of my T-shirt together. My hands were shaking. I couldn't get over my shock. "One minute she was enjoying her dinner. The next . . ."

"Nervous, I guess," Amanda said. "She's just tense. A new house. New people. It must be very frightening to a cat."

I took a deep breath and held it. "She—she *attacked* me. Like a wild animal."

I followed Amanda to the back of the house. I saw the new Bella on the Caplans' bed. She had curled into a ball on one of the pillows. Her eyes were closed. She seemed to be sleeping peacefully. Right at home.

"Like a wild animal," I repeated in a whisper.

Amanda tugged my torn shirt hard. "She needs time to get used to everything. It's a good thing the Caplans won't be back for a few days. By the time they get home, Bella will be perfectly sweet and normal."

I gazed at the black cat curled up so comfy on the Caplans' bed. "Amanda, I sure hope you're right," I said. I tugged her arm. "Come on. Let's get out of here—before she wakes up and attacks again."

"Mickey, you sure spend a lot of time at the Caplans'," Mom said at dinner. "How are you and Amanda getting along with that cat?"

I nearly choked on my chicken leg. That was the *last* question I wanted to be asked tonight.

"Fine," I said. "Everything is perfect."

I had a strong urge to tell Mom and Dad the truth. To tell them everything that had happened today . . .

*We left the Caplans' front door open. Bella ran out and got run over by a truck.*

*Then we stole a black cat from a store and just barely escaped. The cat looks a lot like Bella, so we're hoping to fool the Caplans.*

*But after we fed the new cat tonight, she went berserk and attacked. She leaped on me like a wild creature and raked her claws down the front of my shirt.*

But I was afraid to tell them the truth. And I definitely didn't want them to tell the Caplans what Amanda and I had done.

"If you enjoy this so much," Dad said, "maybe you'll want your own cat."

"Uh . . . maybe," I said.

Later, up in my room, I fed Zorro. I gave him some bits of lettuce and a tiny piece of apple. After his dinner, I tickled his stomach for a little while. He likes that a lot.

He's a very cute mouse. I love the way he gets excited when I come into the room, and he starts to wiggle his nose like crazy till I pet him.

I fed my three goldfish, too. I named them Nick, Joe, and Kevin. Good names for fish.

I did some homework. I texted some of my friends. I tried to call Amanda, but I got her voice mail. I didn't leave a message. She never listens to her messages.

Later in bed, I couldn't get to sleep. I kept thinking about the old Bella and the new Bella. Could Amanda and I really get away with this trick we were pulling on the Caplans?

Thinking about it made my throat tighten. I could feel my dinner churning around in my stomach.

I shut my eyes and tried to concentrate on sleeping. But the harder you concentrate, the more awake you are.

My bedroom window was open. The curtains made a rustling sound as they floated in a soft breeze. In the far distance, I heard a horn honk.

*Relax . . . just relax*, I told myself.

But I gasped and jerked straight up in bed when I heard the sound.

A shrill cat yowl.

From under my bed?

# 15

I grabbed the covers with both hands. Sat up straight and listened.

Silence. Just the soft shifting of the window curtains.

And then—another angry yowl. From beneath the bed.

My heart pounding, I half fell, half leaped out of bed. Dropped to my knees. Pulled up the bedspread and peered under the bed.

No. Too dark.

I climbed to my feet. Fumbled for the lamp on my bed table and clicked it on. Blinking in the yellow light, I dropped back to the floor.

No cat under there.

I saw a lot of dust and a tennis ball and a sneaker I'd been searching for. But no cat.

"I didn't dream it." I said the words out loud. "Where are you, cat?"

Silence.

I sat on the edge of my bed and waited for my heartbeat to slow to normal. My hands and feet were suddenly ice-cold.

My pajama bottoms were twisted. I stood up to straighten them—and heard the cat's shrill cry again.

From across the room?

I jumped up, gazing all around. No sign of a cat.

Could the sound be coming from outside?

I crossed to the window and peered out. Pale moonlight washed over the front yard. It made the bushes and lawn look silvery and unreal.

I didn't see a cat down there.

I grabbed the bottom of the window and pulled it shut. The curtains fell back in place against the wall.

I stood there for a while, frozen. Listening. Listening hard.

Finally, I climbed back into bed. I didn't turn out the light. I pulled the covers up to my chin.

I shut my eyes—and heard the cat's cry again.

"No!" I shouted. "Where are you? Where?"

Did Bella somehow escape the Caplans' house? Did she follow me home?

If she did . . . *why couldn't I see her?*

I climbed out of bed again. I searched the

entire room. Everywhere. Under my desk. Under the pile of dirty clothes on my closet floor. I even opened the dresser drawers and peered inside.

No cat.

I was down on my hands and knees, searching under the bed again, when I remembered a totally scary horror movie Amanda and I had seen at the mall. It was about an evil cat that haunted a family *from inside the walls.*

I was so freaked out by that film, I made my dad move my bed away from the wall.

*Yeeeeoow.*

I heard the cat again. So close. It sounded close enough to reach out and touch.

I spun all around. No cat.

I walked to the wall. I pressed my ear against the red-and-white-striped wallpaper. "Are you in there?" I cried in a trembling voice. I listened. "Are you inside the wall?"

Silence.

*Was I going CRAZY?*

No. No way I was imagining this.

I couldn't stop shivering. My eyes darted around the room as I made my way back to bed. I pulled the covers up again.

I clicked off the bed table light. I scooted down low in the bed. I started to shut my eyes.

*Yeeeeeow.*

"Oh, no!" A cry escaped my throat.

Right above me on the wall . . . a shadow . . . a shadow reflected from the streetlight on the curb.

The shadow of a cat.

# 16

I stared in horror. I don't know how long I stared, not blinking, not moving. Finally, the cat shadow vanished.

I stared at the wall where it had been. Chill after chill ran down my back.

Then ... I heard a soft splash.

What could that be? The bathroom was across the hall. What could splash in my room?

I reached for the lamp and clicked on the light. Across the room, I saw Zorro's cage. Beside it— the fish tank.

Even in the dim light, I could see the water in the tank washing against the sides. Tilting up and down.

I squinted at it, trying to understand. Why was the water splashing in the tank?

I took a deep, shuddering breath. Then I lowered my feet to the floor. I crossed the room and stepped up to the goldfish tank.

Where were my fish?

Too dark to see clearly. I moved to the door and clicked on the ceiling light. I returned to the fish tank . . .

. . . and let out a cry of horror.

The water washed from side to side. And floating on top of the water . . . floating on the top . . . pieces of orange and yellow.

Little chunks of goldfish.

"No!"

I lowered my head over the tank and stared down in shock. I saw a goldfish head on its side with one black eye staring up at me.

The head ended in a jagged yellow line. As if it had been *ripped* off its body.

My three fish had been torn apart. Torn to little hunks.

I saw slender pieces of fin. Tiny bones. Part of a tail. Chunks of yellow-orange washing back and forth in the tilting water.

*Yeeeeeow.*

The cat cry made me jerk straight up. I spun away from the fish tank. My eyes frantically swept over the room.

"Where are you?" I screamed. "What's going on?"

I couldn't see the cat. I could only hear it. And I could see what it had done to my goldfish.

"Where are you?" I screamed again. "Show yourself. Show yourself! What are you doing in my room? What do you *want*?"

# 17

The next morning, Mom and Dad left for work early. So I couldn't tell them about the cat cries and what had happened to my fish. Mom left a box of cereal and the milk at my place at the table. I choked some of it down. But I didn't feel like eating.

I felt groggy. My head weighed at least a hundred pounds. It nearly dropped into my cereal bowl. I kept shaking my head, trying to wake up.

I'm the kind of kid who needs his sleep. Amanda is always bragging about how late she stays up. But if I don't get seven or eight hours, I feel totally weird. Like I've been hit by a truck.

I don't think I had ten minutes of sleep. I was too afraid to close my eyes.

I stayed awake and alert. Waiting for more cat cries. Waiting for the terrifying shadow to appear on my wall again.

Amanda met me on my front stoop and we

started across the lawn to feed Bella. The sun hurt my red, tired eyes. I couldn't stop yawning.

"I—I have to tell you something," I said. "Something scary."

"You won't believe what happened to me last night," Amanda said. "My cousin Reeny came over. You met Reeny, right? Well, she brought this new Wii game. It's a horseback-riding game. It's totally awesome. And the two of us . . ."

I couldn't get Amanda to stop telling me about the game. I kept opening my mouth. But she didn't take a breath. I couldn't get a word in. And I was too tired to shout or clap my hand over her mouth.

"I have something to tell you later," I said, my voice hoarse and weak.

I don't know if she heard me or not. She was still telling me how totally awesome the horseback-riding game was.

We stepped into the Caplans' house—and we had a problem.

We couldn't find Bella.

She wasn't in the living room, waiting to greet us. She wasn't in the kitchen. Amanda and I scrambled around the house, calling her name.

Of course, that was dumb. Her name wasn't really Bella. She didn't *know* her name yet. But we shouted it anyway. And I kept asking if she was hungry. But maybe she didn't know that word, either.

We found her right where we started. She had squeezed under the living room couch. Curled up under there, acting innocent, as if she didn't know two people were frantically running everywhere trying to find her.

Amanda reached down and gently pulled the cat out. She didn't try to resist. Amanda held her in her arms for a few moments. The cat seemed to like it.

"She's getting calmer," Amanda said. "I can tell she's getting used to this house."

"I hope so," I said.

Amanda petted her. "You look so much like Bella," she told the cat. "I'm just going to forget the old Bella ever existed."

I sighed. "We're going to be late for school. I'll give her breakfast."

I walked to the kitchen, pulled the bag of cat food from under the sink, and filled Bella's bowl. "Breakfast!" I shouted. "Are you hungry?"

No cat.

I hurried back to the living room. Bella was still in Amanda's arms. "Let her down so she can eat her breakfast," I said. "We have to get out of here."

"She's in a cuddly mood," Amanda said. But she set the cat down on the floor.

Bella stretched, bending from her middle, poking her tail straight up in the air. She made a soft sound like a yawn.

"Hungry?" I asked her. I motioned to the kitchen. "Hungry? Breakfast? Chow time?"

To my surprise, the cat turned and darted back under the couch.

"She doesn't understand," Amanda said. "Go back in the kitchen and rattle her food dish so she hears it."

I started back for the kitchen—but stopped when I heard a loud noise behind me. "What's that?" I asked Amanda.

Amanda was staring under the couch.

Bella let out an ugly screech. She was on her back. It took me a few seconds to realize what she was doing.

"Oh, no!" I cried. "No! Stop her!"

The cat was scratching frantically on the couch bottom. Screeching like a trapped animal and ripping the bottom of the couch with her claws.

Ripping and clawing faster . . . harder.

"*Do* something!" I shouted to Amanda.

She turned to me, pale, her eyes wide. "Do *what*? I'm not going to try to pull her out."

*Riiiip rippp ripppp.*

"She's pulling all the stuffing out!" I screamed.

Pieces of white foam rubber came flying out from under the couch. And the cat kept scraping out more.

"She's crazy!" I cried. "What's *wrong* with her?"

*Riiiip rippp rippppp.*

Clawing frantically, the cat kept screaming like a maniac.

I dove for the couch and dropped to my knees. I started to reach under the couch with both hands.

*What was I thinking?*

The cat clawed at my hands. She turned her head toward me and, eyes glowing bright yellow, she snapped her teeth.

*"Owwwwww!"*

I jerked my hands away.

Pain shot up my hand and arm. My palm had dark red claw marks down the middle.

I jumped to my feet and backed away. "I—I can't do it. I can't get her out."

Clawing furiously, like a machine out of control, the cat was ripping out the whole bottom of the couch.

"We're going to be really late," Amanda said. "Let's go. Give her time to calm down. Maybe she'll be better if we leave."

"But the mess—" I started.

*Riiiip rippp rippppp.*

"We'll clean it up after school," Amanda said.

She tugged my T-shirt sleeve. "Come on. I can't stand this."

"What's her problem?" I said.

Amanda didn't answer. She was already heading out the front door. I followed her and closed the door behind me.

We stood on the stoop, catching our breath. I could still hear the cat's wild screeches from inside.

I shifted my backpack on my shoulders and started down the steps. I stopped when I saw the three men walking along the sidewalk.

Three men in gray uniforms.

I pulled Amanda off the stoop and behind a tall shrub.

"Look—" I pointed. "He followed us. The guy from Cat Heaven. Lou. And two pals."

We hunched down behind the thick bush.

"It's too late. I think they saw us," Amanda whispered.

# 18

Peeking through the needles of the evergreen shrub, I watched the three men approach. They were walking slowly, studying each house. I felt my throat tighten. I tried to duck lower. My legs were trembling so hard, I almost fell into the bush.

Amanda squeezed my arm. "Why did they follow us?" she whispered. "Why did Lou bring two other guys?"

I couldn't answer her questions. I just shook my head.

I stood very still as they came nearer. They were on the sidewalk, staring up at the Caplans' house.

I realized I was holding my breath. I let it out in a long, silent whoosh.

*Please don't see us. Please keep walking.*

"They have hundreds of cats in their store," Amanda whispered, her mouth right in my ear.

"What's the big deal that we stole one little cat?"

"Shhh." I pressed a finger to my lips.

But she ignored me. "Okay," she whispered. "So we did a bad thing. We stole a cat. But what's the big crime?"

I shrugged. I didn't know the answer.

I only knew I didn't want to be caught. I didn't like the grim looks on the faces of the three men. And I didn't like the way they were staring at the Caplans' house.

Were they coming up the front walk? Did they know the stolen cat was inside?

If they came up here, we were dead meat. They would see us hiding behind the bush.

I held my breath again. And watched them through the prickly evergreen needles.

They squinted up at the front window. Then they started walking again. They walked slowly, side by side, gazing at the next house.

And as they moved on, I heard Lou talking to the others. His words sent a chill down my back:

"We have to find them," he said. "They have no idea the trouble they are in."

# 19

Amanda and I waited behind the bush till Lou and his two partners turned the corner. My face was drenched with sweat. My backpack felt as if it weighed a thousand pounds.

Finally, we crept out and began to walk to school. We stayed behind hedges and walked through backyards. I kept glancing behind us. I was sure the three store clerks would sneak up and grab us.

"M-maybe we should give them back their cat," I stammered. We were across the street from our school. No other kids in sight. We were definitely late.

"We can't do that," Amanda insisted. "You don't want to tell the Caplans what happened to Bella, do you?"

"I—I—" I didn't know what I wanted to do. I just didn't want three angry-looking men searching for me.

"They'll give up and go back to their store,"

Amanda said. "It's just one little cat. It's not such a big deal."

"Then why did they say we don't know the trouble we're in?" I asked.

Amanda shrugged. "Guess they don't like cat thieves."

We crossed the street and ran the rest of the way to the front doors of the school. Miss Harris wasn't in the classroom. So she didn't see us sneak in late.

I dropped my backpack on the floor and sat down in my seat. I mopped the sweat off my forehead with the sleeve of my shirt.

I realized I hadn't told Amanda about the cat sounds in my room last night. The meows and the floating shadows that kept me up all night and what happened to my poor fish.

*I'll tell her at lunch,* I decided.

My friend Aaron sits next to me. He's a big, happy-looking guy with glasses, spiky red hair, and a lot of freckles. Aaron always seems to be grinning. That's his natural expression.

He poked me in the ribs. "What's your problem, Mickey?" he asked. "You look like something the cat dragged in."

"Don't SAY that!" I cried. "Don't mention cats!"

"Well, of course slavery is what divided the states before the Civil War," Miss Harris was saying. "But what was the actual cause of the war? Anybody have an idea? Raise your hand."

Miss Harris is the coolest teacher in our school. She is young and awesome looking with straight blond hair and big blue eyes.

She wears jeans and T-shirts with the names of rock bands on them. And she has a tiny tattoo of a butterfly on the back of one hand.

"Anybody know the direct cause of the war?" she asked. "Let's see some hands. Did you read the chapter?"

I turned my head so Miss Harris wouldn't see me yawning. I couldn't stop yawning all morning. I felt so sleepy, I just wanted to put my head on the desk and conk out.

This was an important morning to be awake and alert. She was starting the Civil War unit this morning.

I should have been taking notes.

But my ears were ringing. And my eyes kept going blurry. And my mouth kept opening in yawn after yawn.

I know I'm only twelve. But like I said, I'm not a night owl. I really need my sleep.

"That's right," Miss Harris was saying. "The root cause of the war was *secession*."

She wrote the word on the whiteboard. "Now we are going to go back in time a little and . . ."

I missed what she said after that because I yawned again. It was taking all my strength to try to hold in my yawns so she wouldn't see them. But it was a losing battle.

I pulled some paper from my backpack and wrote at the top of a fresh page:

*Secession. Root cause.*

I raised my head to see what she was writing on the whiteboard now. And that's when I heard the first meow.

I jumped a mile.

The cat's cry was right behind me.

I spun around hard.

I didn't mean to bump Aaron. But I jerked around so fast, my shoulder crashed into his head, and I almost knocked his glasses off.

"Hey!" he cried out. "What's your problem?"

"Didn't you hear it?" I whispered.

"Is there a problem?" Miss Harris turned to stare at Aaron and me.

*Meeeow.*

"N-no!" I stammered. "No problem."

"Well, Mickey, do you have something you'd like to share with the rest of the class?" she asked.

"No. Sorry," I said. "I . . . uh . . . dropped my pencil."

*Yeeeeow.*

Another cat cry. This time under my seat.

I bent down to find the cat. Nothing under there.

*Yeeeeoww.*

I sat back up. I felt dizzy. The room started to spin.

I heard another cat cry behind me. And then a long, shrill yowl from under my desk again.

I jumped to my feet. I stepped away from the chair. Then I spun around to see the cats.

"Where are they?" I cried. *"Where?"*

Kids turned to stare. A few kids laughed.

"Mickey, what's wrong?" Miss Harris asked. "Are you okay? Sit down, please. Sit down."

*Yeeeoowww.*

"But—don't you hear them?" I cried. "Miss Harris, don't you *hear* them?"

# 20

Kids started to laugh. I guess they thought I was goofing.

Aaron grabbed me and tried to pull me back to my seat. But I missed the chair and landed on my butt on the floor.

That made everyone roar.

I saw Miss Harris laughing along with everyone else. I could feel my face getting hot. I knew I was blushing like crazy.

I was frightened and embarrassed at the same time.

Aaron helped pull me to my feet.

The laughter rang in my ears. But I didn't care about that. I gazed all around, searching for the cat.

Finally, Miss Harris gave the school signal for quiet—two fingers raised above her head. The room grew silent.

*Yeeeoooow.*

I was still on my feet. My legs trembled. My heart was thudding in my chest.

"Don't you hear it?" I repeated, trying to keep my voice steady.

"Hear what, Mickey?" Miss Harris asked. She came down the aisle till she stood right in front of me. "What do you hear? I'm listening. I don't hear anything."

*Yeeeooow.*

"There. It did it again. It's—it's a cat," I stammered. "There's a cat in here. But I can't find it."

She narrowed her blue eyes at me. She frowned. "Is this a dare? Did Aaron dare you to do this?"

Aaron shot both hands up in the air. "No way!" he screamed. "I didn't do anything. He's *crazy*!"

"It's not a dare," I said. I raised my right hand. "I swear."

Miss Harris turned to face the class. "Does anyone else hear a cat? Is Mickey the only one who hears it?"

A few kids laughed. No one raised a hand.

"Amanda, please—" I called. She sits in the front row. I needed her help. "Amanda—do you hear it?"

She shook her head. "I'm sorry, Mickey. I don't hear anything," she said softly. "Maybe . . ." Her voice drifted off. She didn't finish her sentence.

"Everyone look under your seats," Miss Harris said. "Look all around. Find the cat."

She turned back to me and put a hand on my shoulder. "I hope someone finds a cat, Mickey," she said. "I hope you didn't interrupt the Civil War for a joke."

"Not a joke," I muttered.

Chairs scraped as kids looked under their seats. On the other side of the room, two boys cupped their hands around their mouths and meowed.

"Last chance," Miss Harris said. "Does anyone see a cat in here?"

"Yes! I do!" Aaron cried. He pointed under Miss Harris's desk. "I see it! There it is!"

# 21

I gasped and tried to see where he was pointing.

Miss Harris stared at Aaron. "You really see a cat?" she demanded.

"No, actually, I don't," Aaron said. A grin spread over his round, freckled face. "Just messing with you!"

The class erupted in a riot of laughter. Kids hee-hawed and bumped knuckles. A bunch of kids started meowing.

Miss Harris trotted back to the front of the room. She raised her hand in the Quiet signal again. And a few seconds later, the noise stopped.

I saw Amanda staring at me with an unhappy scowl on her face. She motioned with both hands for me to sit down. So I did.

Aaron punched me on the shoulder. "Just funning with you," he said. He giggled.

I forced a smile. I didn't want to fight with him. I didn't want any more trouble of any kind.

Miss Harris sat on the edge of her desk. She glanced up at the big wall clock behind her. "Almost lunchtime," she said. She snapped her notebook shut. "I guess the Civil War will have to take a break till this afternoon. Thanks to Mickey's invisible cat."

Kids stared at me. I lowered my gaze to the floor.

They could stare and laugh all they wanted. Something very scary was going on here, and I was the only one who knew about it.

Even Amanda thought I was going nuts. I had to talk to her. I had to tell her about the shadow on the wall last night. And what happened to my poor fish.

The bell rang. I packed up my stuff and hurried to the lunchroom. Kids meowed at me all down the hall. I laughed and pretended it was all a big joke.

I searched for Amanda in the crowded lunchroom. But she wasn't there yet.

The room smelled of hot dogs and beans. My stomach growled. I could have gone for two or three hot dogs. But Dad packs my lunch every morning. It's always a ham sandwich or tuna salad, a box of juice, and an apple. I throw away all the apples.

I sat down at a table in the corner at the back of the room. No one else around. I watched the door for Amanda.

A huge red-and-yellow poster was strung along the ceiling. It read: SUPPORT THE SNAKES! That's our team name — the South Middle School Rattlesnakes.

Our yearbook is called *The Venom*. Really.

Everyone loves snakes at my school. I think it's kind of weird.

I waited another five minutes. The lunchroom was filling up with kids. I still didn't see Amanda.

I opened my backpack to get my lunch bag. I gazed inside.

My breath caught in my throat. I started to choke.

I stared into the backpack in shock.

Stared at the orange cat gazing up at me.

And as I stared, the cat's eyes began to glow — until they blazed bright red. The lips pulled back, baring yellowed fangs. And the cat opened its mouth wide in a furious *hisssssss*.

# 22

"N-no!"

I tried to scream, but my cry came out in a choked whisper.

The glowing red eyes seemed to burn my face.

I jumped up. Sent my chair toppling onto its back. I staggered away from the table, my eyes on the open backpack.

I spun to the door and saw Amanda enter the lunchroom with two or three other girls. I ran to her, stumbling over a kid's backpack.

"Hey, watch out!" he shouted.

Some kids meowed. Someone threw an empty milk carton at me. It bounced off my shoulder.

"Amanda!" I called breathlessly. "Come here. You—you have to see this. I found the cat!"

I pulled her away from her friends. She gave them a helpless wave. "Catch you later," she called to them.

She turned to me. "What's your problem, Mickey? Why are you freaking out? Are you having a total meltdown?"

"Don't talk," I said. I pulled her through the crowded aisle between tables to the back of the room. "Don't talk, Amanda. Just look."

I grabbed the backpack off the table. I held it up to her and pulled it open so she could see inside.

She lowered her eyes. Blinked a few times. Gazed into the backpack. And uttered a startled cry. "Wow," she murmured. "Mickey — wow."

# 23

"I don't see anything," Amanda said. "Am I missing the joke?"

"J-joke?" I stammered. I jerked the backpack away from her and gazed inside.

I saw my binder, a few books, and my brown lunch bag.

"But—but—" I sputtered. "There was a cat in there. Listen to me, Amanda. When I opened it, I—I saw an orange cat. It must be the one I kept hearing in class. And—"

"Sit down," she said sharply. She grabbed my arm and pulled me down to a chair. Then she dropped into the chair beside me.

"What's up, Mickey? You've been totally berserk all morning."

I slid the backpack closer and dug my hand around in it. "I'm not making it up," I said.

"Just tell me what's going on," Amanda insisted.

Some girls from our class waved to her at the next table. But she kept her eyes locked on me.

I shoved the backpack across the table. "I—I don't know what's going on," I stammered. "It started last night."

I told her how I kept hearing a cat meow in my room. And how I searched everywhere and couldn't find it. I told her about the shadow. And about my goldfish. How I found chunks of fish floating at the top of the tank.

Amanda made a disgusted face. She stuck out her tongue. *"Bleccccch."*

"It's not a joke. It really happened," I said. "And I didn't tell you the weirdest thing of all."

She squinted hard at me. "You're not making this up? You're not trying to scare me?"

I raised my right hand. "I swear."

She pressed her hand to my forehead, pretending to take my temperature.

"Then I kept hearing a cat in class this morning," I said. "That's why I jumped up like that. Maybe it was the cat in my backpack. I'm not making any of this up. I'm totally freaking out, Amanda."

She stared at me. "You're just stressed and upset," she said finally.

"Upset?"

"Yes. Because of the switch we pulled with Bella," Amanda said. "First, the cat was killed.

The cat we were responsible for. That's very upsetting, right?"

"Right," I agreed.

"Then you stole a black cat from the pet store."

"*I* stole it?" I cried. "I thought *we* stole it."

"Yes, but *you* did the actual running out the door stealing thing," Amanda replied. "And I think you're very messed up about that."

"True," I said. "And then the new Bella acts totally weird. Sweet and gentle one minute. Then like a fiendish monster the next minute."

Amanda nodded her head. "Yes. And it all has you totally wired and freaked out," she said.

"So?"

"So . . . that explains why you're hearing cats all the time, Mickey. And why you're seeing cats everywhere."

"I get it," I said. "You think I'm crazy."

"Not crazy. Stressed," she replied. "Totally stressed."

"You're wrong, Amanda," I said. "I'm not imagining any of these things. What about my goldfish? Do you think I chewed my own goldfish to pieces? I'm not imagining any of this. It's real. It's all real."

She stood up. She patted my shoulder. "If it's all real, Mickey, how come you're the only one who heard the cat in class this morning?"

My mouth dropped open. I wanted to answer that. But I had no answer.

"I have to get some lunch," Amanda said. She patted my shoulder again. "Take a deep breath. You'll be fine."

I rolled my eyes. "Awesome advice," I muttered. But she was already on her way to the lunch line.

*Okay,* I thought, *so she doesn't believe me.*

*She'd believe me if I showed her what was floating in my goldfish tank.*

I started to feel a little angry. I mean, this whole cat switch was Amanda's idea. And now she didn't want to hear what was really going on. She just wanted to believe that I was imagining things.

I realized my stomach was growling again. I slid the backpack closer. I peered inside before I reached in and tugged out the brown paper lunch bag.

I started to unfold the bag. But I stopped when I felt something weird. Something lumpy and hard inside the bag.

A sour aroma floated out. Something *stank.*

I reached inside and wrapped my fingers around it. I tugged it out—and tried to scream.

But it's impossible to scream and gag at the same time.

A dead mouse.

My hand was wrapped around a dead gray mouse.

Its body was stiff and hard. Its eyes had sunk into their sockets. I saw deep bite marks on its back.

The smell was sickening.

The mouse fell from my trembling hand. It thudded on the table and bounced onto the floor.

I jumped to my feet. Was the dead mouse a gift from the cat? It was the kind of present a cat would leave.

I couldn't think straight. I knew I couldn't eat. I smelled my hand. It reeked of dead mouse.

I tossed the lunch bag in the trash. Then I hurried out of the lunchroom. I heard Aaron calling me. I just waved to him and kept walking.

I didn't really know where I was going. I needed to find someplace quiet and try to figure this out.

Or maybe I needed to tell someone what was happening. Maybe tell my parents the whole truth.

I had gym right after lunch. I wandered into the gym. But no one was there yet.

Two volleyball nets had been set up in the middle of the floor. Bright lights made the polished floor gleam.

For a moment, I thought I saw someone sitting in the bleachers at the far end. But it was just a blue jacket someone had draped over a bench.

I made my way to the locker room to change into my gym clothes.

I pulled open the door and stepped inside. About twenty degrees hotter in here. The locker room air smelled damp and sweaty.

I felt something soft under my shoe.

"Ohhh!" What did I step on?

A cat?

No.

I jumped back. A balled-up pair of gym socks.

*Take it easy, Mickey.*

*Maybe Amanda is right about you.*

I heard water dripping in the shower room. "Anybody in here?" I shouted. My voice echoed off the tile walls.

No reply.

My locker was near the back, across from the shower room. I stepped up to it and grabbed the combination lock. I started to turn the combination—then stopped.

I knew what I'd find inside the locker. A cat.

I started to tremble. I just stood there with both hands on the combination lock. Afraid to turn it. Afraid to open the little gym locker.

I took a deep, shuddering breath. I forced my hands to stop shaking. And I spun the dial to the three combination numbers.

Another deep breath. Then I tugged off the lock and swung the locker door open.

"Noooooo!"

I screamed as it came tumbling out.

It jumped out—bounced off my chest—and onto my knee.

# 25

No. Not a cat.

Not a cat. One of my black-and-white gym sneakers.

It bounced off my knee and thudded to the floor.

"Oh, wow." I shook my head. I balled my hands into fists. I felt so angry at myself for being in a total panic.

Even a gym sneaker *terrified* me.

I dropped onto the nearest bench and waited for my heartbeat to slow down to normal. I picked up the sneaker and rolled it around in my hands.

Weird. Something was tucked inside of the shoe.

*Oh, nooo.* Something feathery and gray.

I pulled it out. And with a loud cry, tossed it across the locker room.

A dead bird. A sparrow with its head dangling by a thread.

Another gift from a cat?

I jumped to my feet, tossed the sneaker into the locker, and slammed the door shut. The sound echoed through the empty room.

Then I heard a cat's yowl. A long, shrill *yeeeooow* that sent a chill down my back.

"No! Shut up!" I screamed. "*Shut up!* Go away! Leave me alone!"

"*Yeeeeoowwwwww.*"

Right behind me.

I spun around. No cat there.

"Leave me alone!" I cried. I clapped my hands over my ears.

But even with my ears covered, I could hear the yowls and cries of the cats. Not just one. Several cats now. All meowing and yowling at once.

The terrifying cries rang from all around me.

I pressed my hands tighter against the sides of my face, as if trying to force them away. But it seemed to only make their cries louder and more frightening.

"Where *are* you?" I screamed. "Why are you following me?"

I had to get out of there. I had to find help.

I lurched toward the locker room door. But I tripped over something.

A cat? A cat I couldn't see?

I landed hard on my knees on the concrete floor. Pain shot up my legs.

*Meeeeeyowwwww!*

And then the yowling turned to hisses. Angry hisses all around me.

So close. So close.

The hisses came at me in a steady rhythm. As if all the invisible cats were breathing together.

I couldn't scream. I couldn't breathe. Or move.

Invisible cats. I was surrounded by angry, invisible cats.

I shut my eyes. I wanted to be far away.

When I opened them, the cats were standing in front of me. I could SEE them!

How many were there? Eight? No. Ten? More! Scrawny. Their fur matted and tangled, with patches of skin showing through holes in the fur.

Their eyes glowed bright yellow. Like monsters in a horror movie. Their open mouths revealed pointed yellow fangs.

They formed a circle around me. Their backs arched. Their fur stood on end.

I raised my arms to shield myself. But what could I do against so many hissing, angry cats?

They all pounced at once.

Flung their claws in the air and leaped at me from every side.

"HELP me!" I managed to scream before I went down. Before I sank to the floor beneath the hissing, snapping, clawing attackers.

"HELP me! Can anyone HEAR me? I need HELP!"

# 26

On my back now, I wrestled with them. Struggled to push them off me.

Their fur was dry and bristly. And their bodies felt COLD.

"Help me!" I tried to choke out a scream. But a cat leaped onto my face and pressed its cold belly over my mouth and nose.

I shoved it away. Sucked in a deep breath.

And heard a pounding sound. Someone pounding on the locker room door.

"Who's in there?" a man called. "Who locked this door?"

I recognized his voice. Mr. Weston, the gym teacher. Mr. Weston is a big guy with a huge stomach, shaggy long hair, and a bushy mustache. He's totally out of shape. He doesn't look anything like a gym teacher.

But I was sure glad to hear him out there.

His fists boomed on the door again. "Who locked this? Open up!"

At the sound of his voice, the cats froze. They all stiffened as if frightened. Their glowing eyes dulled until they were dark. The eyes appeared to sink into their sockets.

The cats scrambled off me. They ran with their heads down, scraggly tails trailing behind them. Into the shower room at the back wall.

I sat up. I brushed myself off furiously. Cat fur flew into the air.

I was gasping for breath. Breathing so hard, my chest hurt.

Mr. Weston pounded again on the locker room door. Each blow thundered through the room. "Who is in there? Who locked this?"

I forced myself to my feet. I staggered to the door on trembling legs.

I turned the lock. The door swung open fast. I had to jump back to keep from being hit.

The gym teacher stood staring at me. Several kids were bunched up behind him.

"Mickey?" He couldn't hide his surprise. "What's going on? You look a mess. What were you doing in here?"

"Cats," I managed to say in a tiny, weak voice. "The cats—" I pointed to the shower room.

He squinted at me. "Cats?"

I turned and motioned for him to follow me. I led the way to the shower room.

Of course, I knew the cats wouldn't be there when we looked in.

And they weren't.

I waited for the other guys in my class to change their clothes. When they ran to the gym to play volleyball, I stepped up to the locker room mirror.

To my surprise, I had only a few scratches.

I pulled a wad of orange cat fur from my hair. It made me shudder. I glanced around the locker room, expecting the hissing cats to return.

I felt a hand on my shoulder. Mr. Weston gazed down at me. "Mickey, are you coming out for class?"

"I—I don't think so," I said. "I . . . don't feel too great."

He nodded. "Well, you can come out and watch," he said. "Or do you want to see the nurse?"

"The nurse can't help me," I muttered.

He nodded again, turned, and walked out of the locker room.

*The nurse can't help me*, I thought. *Who can? Who can I talk to about my cat problem?*

Amanda was the only one who knew about Bella and what we did at Cat Heaven. But even she didn't believe me when I told her I was being *haunted* by cats.

I knew I had to talk to her. She had to help me. She had to believe me.

The afternoon dragged and dragged. It felt like everything was moving in slow motion.

Miss Harris started the Civil War again. I tried to take notes, but I just couldn't think straight.

Every noise made me jump. Every high voice or cry or laugh in the classroom made me think the cats were back.

I couldn't sit still. I couldn't stop shaking my legs and tapping the desktop with both hands. I kept alert, gazing under chairs and desks, looking for cats. I expected a cat to attack me any moment.

I'd never been so stressed and jumpy in my life.

When the bell rang, I left my books and backpack and ran across the room to Amanda. "We—we need to talk," I said breathlessly. "About the cat."

"Not now," she said. She turned away and began to stuff things into her backpack. Then she began to paw through her big canvas bag. "Where did I put my bus pass?"

"Bus pass? Where are you going?" I cried. "I'm desperate. I have to talk to you."

She made a face at me. "You know I have my flute lesson today."

"Skip it," I said.

"I can't skip it," she insisted, pulling out the bus pass. "Our recital is Sunday, and I've got to practice. Bach is really hard, you know."

"I don't know about Bach," I said. "I only know I'm being haunted. I think—I think we have to take Bella back to Cat Heaven."

"No way!" Amanda said, pushing me away. "Later, okay? Save your ghost stories for tonight. You're going to make me late."

She tossed both bags over her shoulder and ran out of the classroom.

I stood there staring until she disappeared. *Ghost stories?*

This wasn't a ghost story. This was real. This was my life.

Shaking my head, I gathered up my stuff and headed out into the hall. Some guys at their lockers turned and meowed at me.

I laughed, pretending it was funny. Showing them I'm a good guy and can take a joke.

Some joke.

The sound of their meows made my stomach tighten.

I walked past a group of cheerleaders in their red-and-yellow uniforms. They were practicing a cheer as they walked to the gym.

I stepped outside into a cool, gray afternoon. Low clouds overhead. I felt a raindrop and then another raindrop on my forehead.

I was walking past the soccer field, nearly to the street, when I saw the three men in gray work uniforms. Lou and his two buddies. Standing together on the grass.

I glanced around. I was out in the open. Nowhere to hide.

Did they recognize me?

Yes.

All three men began waving wildly as they came racing across the soccer field toward me.

"Hey, you!" Lou shouted. He stuck his arm straight out and pointed at me. "Freeze! Stop right there!"

# 27

Should I talk to them? Or run?

I wanted this to be over. I wanted to tell someone the whole story.

But the angry looks on their faces told me they wouldn't want to listen. They wanted to punish me for stealing.

So I ran.

I darted into the street. Tires squealed. A car swerved to avoid me. The driver sent out a long, angry horn blast.

I froze in panic in the middle of the street. I glanced around. No way to escape them if I ran down the block. They were too close and coming on fast.

"Hey, stop! Wait right there, kid!"

They were shouting and waving, their feet pounding the pavement. Then they leaped off the curb, onto the street.

My breath came out in short wheezes. My

heart fluttered in my chest. I was so frightened, I bit my tongue.

"*Owww.*" The sharp pain moved me into action.

I spun around. And dodged between two parked SUVs. I sprinted between a bunch of kids on bikes. And raced toward the school building.

*I'll be safe there*, I told myself. *Safer than on the street.*

*They won't follow me into the school.*

*And there are plenty of places to hide in there.*

"Stop!" Lou shouted behind me. "You're in big trouble! Stop right now!"

"Somebody grab that kid!"

I heard people screaming. I saw some startled parents who had come to pick up their kids. They backed away as I ran past.

The shouts and cries faded as I grabbed the entrance doors to the school building, hurtled inside, and shut them behind me.

Where to hide?

I tore down the empty hall, past rows of gray lockers and dark classrooms.

Over my wheezing breath I could hear the cheerleaders practicing downstairs in the gym. And I heard music — a march. The band rehearsing in the music room.

*I'm safe here. They won't follow me into the school.*

I gasped as I heard shouts behind me. Heavy, pounding footsteps.

I nearly fell over as I swung to look behind me. Lou and his two pals. They were stampeding down the hall.

"Freeze!"

"Stop right there! Don't run away!"

"Stop, kid!"

Their voices echoed off the gray tile walls.

Why were they so desperate to catch me? I stole a cat. But so what? Do they send *three guys* out to capture everyone who takes a cat without paying?

"You're in trouble, kid!"

"Stop! Just stop!"

I knew I was in trouble. They didn't have to tell me that.

I spun around a corner. Running off balance, I slid on the linoleum floor. I skidded to a stop when I saw someone had left a locker open.

I didn't even think about it. I darted into the locker.

I squeezed into the narrow metal locker, spun around to face the front—and shut the door.

I didn't mean to slam it so hard. It made a loud *clannng.*

Did they hear it? Could they hear my gasping breaths?

I shut my eyes and listened. Their shoes thudded on the hard floor. Their angry shouts boomed like bellowing animals.

I heard them turn the corner. They kept running.

"Where is he?" I heard Lou shout.

"Keep going," one of his pals replied. "I saw him run this way."

I had my eyes shut, fingers crossed. I gritted my teeth. And listened to them run right past the locker.

I let out a long whoosh of air. My heart wouldn't stop pumping and thumping. So loud I could barely hear their fading footsteps.

My face was drenched in sweat. I suddenly realized it was hot inside this locker. My legs ached. I tried to shift my weight. I was standing on someone's books and papers.

A metal hook dug into my back. I leaned forward, but there wasn't room to get away from the hook.

I pressed my ear against the locker door. I listened for the three men to return. To come running back down the hall.

Would they search the lockers to find me? Were they *that* desperate?

Silence now.

I waited. Waited.

So cramped and hot and uncomfortable in the narrow space. My back started to itch. Sweat trickled into my eyes.

*Time to get out of here,* I decided. *They're not coming back.*

I fumbled for the door latch.

I grabbed it and pulled up. It didn't budge.

I tried to jiggle it. No. It wouldn't move.

Maybe I had the wrong piece of the latch. I squinted down at the door. Too dark to see anything.

I brushed my hand over the metal gears down there. Tried to pull the latch up. Tried to push it down.

My hand found some kind of round gear. I gripped it tightly and tried to spin it. One way. Then the other.

No. It didn't spin.

I edged my shoulder against the door. Tried to move the latch and push the door out with my shoulder.

No.

I brushed sweat from my eyes. My legs were trembling.

I listened. No one in the hall.

I couldn't call out for help. Lou and his two partners might hear me.

I couldn't shout. And I couldn't budge the latch.

I was trapped inside this thing. Trapped with the hook poking into my back. And my legs trembling. And sweat rolling down my face.

Trapped in this locker the size of a coffin.

# 28

My back ached. The sides of the locker squeezed my shoulders.

I tried to squirm into a more comfortable position. But there was no room to move.

My hand wrapped around the latch once again. I tried pulling it. Pushing it. Twirling it.

I heard footsteps. I sucked in a lungful of air and held it. And listened.

Light footsteps scraping the floor.

I peeked out through the narrow air slots in the door. I saw a flash of blond hair across the hall. I squinted till I saw the kid's face.

Greg Baum. A fourth-grader I knew from Sunday school.

"Hey, Greg—" I whispered through the air vent.

He kept walking.

"Greg—stop!" I called a little louder.

I could see him spin around. His eyes bulged in surprise. "Who's there?"

"Greg—it's me. Mickey Coe. I'm inside a locker."

"Huh? Why?" he asked.

"Because I got stuck," I said. "I'm locked in. Can you let me out?"

I kept talking until Greg found the locker. Then he opened the door without any trouble.

I came tumbling out. I stumbled all the way to the wall across from us. I hit the wall and bounced off.

Greg studied me. "Why did you shut yourself in that locker?"

"It was kind of a dare thing," I lied.

He started to ask more questions. But I took off. No sign of the three cat store dudes. So I ran straight to the front of the school, shoved open the doors, and burst outside.

I glanced up and down the street. No. I didn't see them.

The rain had stopped, and the afternoon sun was sinking behind the trees. I tried to stay in the long shadows as I ran.

All the way home, I kept turning and checking behind me. I kept expecting them to jump out from behind a tree or the side of a house.

It was only three blocks. But it was a terrifying run. I darted through backyards and along a narrow alley filled with trash cans.

Were they still searching the school?

107

I could see they wouldn't give up. They were going to chase after me till they caught me.

And then ... *what*? Turn me over to the police?

I had to talk to Amanda. We had to make a plan.

Thinking about Amanda made me remember the cat. I couldn't run straight home. I had to stop and feed Bella first.

By the time I reached the Caplans' house, I was exhausted, dripping with sweat, and still terrified. I found the keys in my backpack and unlocked the front door. I reached for the doorknob—and stopped.

A chill of fear ran down my back.

I pictured the cat leaping onto me, claws outstretched. Hissing. Screeching. Scratching and biting.

Was she waiting for me? Ready to pounce?

I swallowed. My hand trembled as I grabbed the knob again.

I knew I had no choice. I had to go in the house. I had to feed her and clean her litter box.

Maybe Bella had calmed down. Maybe she was used to her new home. Maybe she would be a nice, gentle cat from now on.

I turned the knob and pushed the door open just a few inches. I stuck my head inside and peered into the front hallway. "Bella?"

She was sitting there, a few feet from the front door. She sat up straighter when she saw me. Her eyes appeared to light up.

"Bella?" I stepped into the hall and carefully closed the door behind me. "Are you going to be a good cat?" I said softly.

She answered with a deafening screech. Raised her front claws—and leaped at me, snapping her jaws.

"Noooo!"

This time, I wasn't surprised. I was ready for her.

As she jumped, I shot out both hands. I caught her around the middle before she could land on me.

She screeched and squirmed and clawed. But I gripped her tightly and held her in the air.

I struggled to hold on. But I saw something that made the breath catch in my throat. I started to choke.

The cat fell from my hands.

I staggered back, staring . . . staring at something *impossible*.

"Noooo!" The cry burst from deep inside me. "No! It can't be. I—I don't *believe* it!"

# 29

I stared in shock at the cat's tail. At the chunk of missing fur on her tail.

I pictured Amanda's bubble gum stuck to the *first* Bella's tail. Amanda had to cut the gum off with a pair of scissors.

The first Bella had a circle of fur missing.

But that Bella was dead.

So how did this cat have the *same chunk of fur* missing in the exact same place on her tail?

As I stared at the pink circle of skin, I felt a cold shudder run down my back.

"It—it's impossible," I murmured to myself. "No way..."

The cat raised her head and gazed up at me with glowing yellow eyes.

*It can't be the same cat,* I thought, staring back at it. *But she looks just like the first Bella. And the same spot of fur is missing.... YIKES!*

This was too frightening for me. Suddenly, I knew what I had to do.

Bella followed me as I began to search the house. I pulled open closet doors. I searched under beds and behind couches.

Finally, I found what I was looking for. A cat carrier, folded up at the back of a linen closet.

I pulled it out and unfolded it. I opened the canvas door on the side and set the carrier down on the floor.

"Go ahead, Bella," I said, pointing. "Get inside. Go."

To my surprise, she stepped right into the carrier. I reached down quickly and fastened the door behind her. I could see her eyes glowing in there like two fireflies.

I carried the case to the front door. Then I set it down. I didn't really want to do this alone.

I pulled out my phone and tried Amanda's number. It rang and rang. Finally, I got her voice mail.

"Never mind," I said. And I hung up.

Okay. I *was* going to do this by myself. I didn't want to wait. I knew it had to be done.

I carried the case to the bus stop. Bella had grown very still inside it.

I peered in through the screen. She was curled up in a tight ball, her tail wrapped around her legs.

"Good," I murmured. I felt relieved that she wasn't giving me a hard time. No screeching or hissing or clawing at the sides of the carrier.

Taking her back to Cat Heaven was hard enough.

I knew that Lou and the other store clerks were really angry. I expected them to give me a hard time.

I was ready to face them. I had broken the law. I stole the cat. I deserved to be in trouble.

I just hoped they wouldn't call the police.

The bus ride took forever. I sat in the backseat with the cat carrier on my lap. Bella didn't raise her head. The carrier seemed to grow heavier and heavier.

The bus driver got into a yelling fight with the driver of a red SUV. He stopped the bus and jumped out to scream at her.

I just wanted to get this afternoon over with. Horns honked. People shouted. Finally, the driver climbed back into his seat, and the bus started up again.

By the time I reached Cat Heaven, the sun had almost set. My heart started to pound as I crossed the parking lot.

A man in denim work overalls came out of the store dragging an enormous red bag of kitty litter. He heaved it onto the back of his pickup truck.

He turned to me. "What've you got in there, son? A cat?"

I raised the carrier. "Yeah. I'm returning it," I said.

He climbed into the front of his truck. I was glad he didn't want to see the cat or ask me any more questions.

I stepped up to the entrance. A sign by the door read: 2 FOR 1 SALE. Did that mean two cats for the price of one?

The glass doors slid open. I took a deep breath and stepped into the store.

The lemony smell of air freshener and cat litter greeted me.

I heard a cat yowl. Then a few more cats joined in.

Standing at the entrance, it took me a little while to realize what was happening.

Then I gasped as the cats started to go *nuts*.

The whole store came alive at once. Hundreds and hundreds of cats began to scream and yowl and cry. The sound rose up in front of me, a wall of wails and angry screeches.

I stared at the cages in the first row. Screaming cats threw themselves at their cage bars. They clawed the sides and tops of their cages. They climbed the cage walls. They flung themselves at the doors, trying to break out.

I staggered back against the wall.

I had to set the cat carrier down and cover my ears against the deafening wails and cries.

*Did I cause this?* I asked myself.

*Is this cat riot my fault?*

I didn't have time to think about it.

Lou and the two gray-uniformed store clerks came running down the aisle. Their faces were red. They were pointing at me angrily.

Cats yowled and howled and flung themselves at their cages, wild-eyed, drooling.

I froze in fear and total confusion.

Lou grabbed me by the shoulder. "I've got you!" he screamed over the racket.

He shoved the cat carrier into my hands—and dragged me out the front door.

# 30

The glass doors slid shut behind us. I could still hear the cats carrying on in the store.

Lou and the two other men formed a tight circle around me. Their faces were grim and angry. Lou had his eyes on the cat carrier in my hands.

I raised it to him. "I — I brought her back," I stammered in a tiny, frightened voice. "I — I'm so sorry I stole her."

I tried to push the carrier into his hands.

But to my surprise he shoved it back at me.

"That's why we've been chasing after you," he said. "That's why we've been trying to catch you. I had to tell you *you can't bring the cat back.*"

"Huh?" A gasp escaped my throat. I still had the cat carrier held high in front of me. "What did you just say?"

"You can't bring her back," Lou said. "Get away from here. And take that cat with you."

"You can't bring that dead cat back here," one of the other clerks said.

*Dead cat?*

"Don't come anywhere near here with her," Lou said. "Go away. Now. I'm warning you."

"But—but—" I sputtered.

The three men held tense fists at their sides and glared at me.

"Go," Lou muttered through gritted teeth.

My head was spinning. The clerk's words kept swimming through my mind.

*"You can't bring that dead cat back here."*

Gripping the cat carrier tightly, I turned and ran. My shoes slapped the asphalt parking lot. I ran without seeing, without thinking.

I just heard those terrifying words over and over.

Did I really have a dead cat in my hands?

I saw Bella get run over by that truck. How could she be back?

I could still hear the yowls of the cats inside the store. I reached the bus stop and glanced back. The three men were still standing in the parking lot, watching me.

They wanted to make sure I left. Why were they so afraid?

I had only questions. No answers.

When the bus finally came, I climbed on and took my seat in the very back. I set the carrier down gently on my lap.

The bus started up. I brought my face close to the screen on the carrier. Bella was sitting up, staring out at me calmly.

"Are you really dead?" I asked her softly.

She brought her face up against the screen and tried to lick my hand.

Amanda was waiting on the front stoop of the Caplans' house. "Where did you go?" she asked. "Why did you take the cat?"

"We have to talk," I said. "It's too weird. It's all too weird."

I set the carrier down. Bella let out a soft cry.

Amanda squatted down to see Bella. "Is she okay?"

"I—I don't think so," I said. "I mean, I don't really know. I took her back to Cat Heaven."

"You *what*?" Amanda cried.

"They wouldn't take her back," I said. "They've been searching for us all this time to tell us we can't return her."

"That's crazy," Amanda said.

"That's not the crazy part," I said. "Here's the crazy part. They told me this cat is dead."

To my surprise, Amanda burst out laughing.

"I really believed you for a moment," she said. She slapped my shoulder. "You got me. You looked as serious as an artichoke!"

"I *am* serious," I told her. "It isn't a joke."

"You're saying there's a dead cat looking out

at us from this carrier case?" Amanda demanded. "Bella Two is a dead cat? Some kind of zombie?"

I shrugged. "That's what they told me. And they weren't joking. They were totally serious."

"Do you have the Caplans' key?" Amanda said. "Let's go inside and talk about this."

I unlocked the front door, picked up the cat carrier, and followed Amanda inside.

"Oh, nooo!" I uttered a cry.

We both stopped in the doorway and cried out in shock.

The living room was *filled* with cats.

# 31

Two cats sprawled on the couch. One sat on the coffee table. Another cat had climbed on top of the TV. Two sat on the carpet in front of us.

They were scrawny and mean looking. Hunched. Their fur ragged and patchy. One of them had only half a tail. The cat perched on the TV was missing an eye.

Inside the carrier, Bella let out a screech. She began to claw furiously at the side. The door popped open—and Bella came shooting out.

The cats tossed back their heads and began to yowl. They jumped off the furniture and began to circle Amanda and me. They eyed us menacingly. Bared their fangs and hissed.

"Do you see them?" I cried.

Amanda grabbed my shirtsleeve. "Yes. I see them. Where did these cats come from?" she cried. "What are they *doing* here?"

"I—I don't know," I stammered. "Maybe—maybe they're *all dead*!"

Bella arched her back and screeched at the circling cats. The black fur on her back stood straight up. She screeched again and again.

"Let's get *out* of here!" I cried.

Amanda and I spun away from them. We started for the front door.

And the door swung open in front of us.

"Hey!" I cried out.

Mrs. Caplan came walking in.

She wore a short-sleeved red T-shirt over a long-sleeved yellow T-shirt and a short purple skirt. She had her dark hair tied up in a purple bandanna. When she saw the ragged cats, her dark eyes bulged. She dropped the suitcase she'd been carrying.

Mr. Caplan came in right behind her, lugging two suitcases. He wore a red-and-yellow Hawaiian shirt and white tennis shorts.

"We came home a few days early—" he said. But then his mouth dropped open. His eyes blinked behind his round eyeglasses. "What's going *on* in here?" he cried.

"Where did these cats come from? Where is Bella?" Mrs. Caplan demanded in her booming voice.

I pointed. Bella had crawled under the couch. She was hissing at the other cats.

Mr. Caplan bent down and picked Bella up. He soothed her, holding her tightly against his chest.

The other cats grew quiet. They stopped prowling and gazed up at the Caplans.

"How did they get in here?" Mrs. Caplan demanded.

"I . . . have to tell you the whole story," I said. "Amanda and I . . . well . . . we're really sorry."

"Sorry?" she asked.

"We left the front door open," Amanda said. "Bella ran out and got run over by a truck. So . . . I got this great idea that didn't turn out so great."

"We went to that pet store, Cat Heaven," I said. "And we brought home this substitute cat. We—we thought maybe we could fool you into thinking it was the real Bella."

"We know it was a terrible thing to do," Amanda said.

"And we're so—so sorry," I said again. "We messed up. It's totally our fault."

Mrs. Caplan put a hand on my shoulder. "Don't be sorry, Mickey," she said. "We should have told you the truth."

I squinted at her. "The truth?"

She nodded. "Yes. Bella was a dead cat from the beginning. Bella died four years ago."

# 32

The Caplans shooed the scraggly cats out of the way. They sat down on the couch. Mr. Caplan still held Bella in his arms.

Amanda and I stood awkwardly in the center of the room. We waited for them to explain.

"I'll make this short and sweet," Mr. Caplan said, petting Bella. "Four years ago, Bella ran out of the house and was run over by a truck. But we couldn't bear to part with her. Then someone told us about the place where cats who die violent deaths go — Cat Heaven."

Amanda and I both gasped. "It isn't a store?" I said. "It *really* is cat heaven?"

"The cats in front are live cats," Mr. Caplan said. "But the cats in the back room are dead. They appear alive in every way. You bring them home, and they are fine. The problem is, if they get out of the house, they reenact their violent death."

I stared hard at him. "You mean —"

"Bella ran out of the house three times before," Mrs. Caplan said, shaking her head sadly. "Each time, she was run over by a truck. Then we had to go back to Cat Heaven to bring her home again."

"But what are these other cats?" Mr. Caplan demanded. "Are they dead, too? What are they doing here?"

"I—I think they escaped when I stole Bella," I stammered. "I grabbed Bella and ran out the back door. I knocked cages over. These cats must have escaped, too. They followed me. They've been *haunting* me!"

"Oh, wow." Mr. Caplan shook his head. "That's bad, Mickey. That's really bad."

"Don't you realize what you've done?" Mrs. Caplan's face had gone pale. Her chin trembled. "Don't you realize you've *ruined your life*?"

# 33

I stared at her. I couldn't speak. I wanted to ask her why she said that. But I couldn't find any words.

Mr. Caplan sat petting Bella. He kept his eyes on the cat. He didn't look at me.

The other cats padded closer to me. They watched me, as if they expected something from me. A gray cat with half its tail missing brushed against my leg.

"You can't just walk in and take a dead cat from the back room at Cat Heaven," Mrs. Caplan explained finally. "Only the cat's *true owner* can carry it out of the store. Only a cat's true owner can claim it."

"If the dead cat is taken out by the wrong owner, it will become evil," Mr. Caplan said, shaking his head. "Bella is gentle now. But she will become angry and wildly, fiercely evil."

"I — I know," I muttered.

"We had a lot of trouble with her," Amanda said.

"You've upset the whole cat universe," Mr. Caplan continued.

"These other dead cats belong to you now, Mickey," Mrs. Caplan said. "You let them out. They will haunt you. They will stay with you forever."

"They—they've been following me everywhere," I stammered. "Giving me presents. Then attacking me."

She sighed. "Poor boy. You—you didn't know what you were doing. But now these cats will haunt you for the rest of your life."

"No!" I cried. "No way! That can't be!"

The gray cat brushed my leg again. It sent chills up my body. The other cats stood stiffly, staring up at me.

"What can I do?" I demanded. "I—I'll round them up and take them back to Cat Heaven."

"You can't take them back," Mr. Caplan said softly. "The store won't take them back."

I pictured Lou out in the parking lot. Telling me to take Bella away and never come back.

"But . . . I can't. . . . These cats . . . I . . ."

I couldn't talk. I couldn't think straight.

"I'm so so so sorry," Mrs. Caplan said. "We never thought this would happen."

"There must be something Mickey can do," Amanda said in a trembling voice.

The Caplans both shook their heads sadly.

Suddenly, I had an idea.

I rushed to the front door and pulled it wide open. Then I motioned to the cats. "Go! Out the door! All of you—GO!"

They stared up at me without moving.

"Go!" I screamed, waving my arms wildly. "Out the door! Beat it! Get lost! Go!"

No.

They didn't move. They didn't even turn their heads to the door.

Failure.

I let out a long, weary sigh.

Suddenly, I had a *better* idea.

# 34

I turned and darted out of the house. I crossed the lawn to my house. Ran upstairs to my room.

My brain was whirring. I could almost hear it spinning.

I pulled the top off Zorro's glass cage and carefully picked the little guy up. I brushed some wood shavings off his fur. The mouse twitched his nose and gazed up at me with his little black-dot eyes.

"I'm sorry, Zorro," I told him. "I'm really going to miss you, fella. But I need you to save my life today."

I cupped him in my hands and ran back to the Caplans' house.

I was heartbroken. I didn't want to lose Zorro. He was an awesome pet.

But I couldn't be more desperate. My life depended on this. He was my only hope. My only hope of not having to spend my life haunted by a dozen scraggly, vicious dead cats.

I carried him into the living room. No one had moved. The Caplans sat on the couch, shaking their heads, murmuring to each other. Mr. Caplan had Bella in his lap. Amanda stood leaning against the back of an armchair.

The dead cats all turned to watch me. I raised Zorro high so they could see him.

"What are you doing?" Amanda demanded. "Why did you bring your mouse?"

"Just watch," I said. "I hope—I hope this works."

I pulled the front door open wide. Then I swung Zorro around so the dead cats could all see him again.

Then I lowered the little white mouse to the floor. Gave him a light push. And sent him scampering to the door.

I turned to the cats. "Go get him!" I cried. "Chase him! Get him! GO!"

Again, they stared up at me. Again, they didn't move.

"Get the mouse! Chase the mouse!" I screamed. "Go, go, GO!"

I turned and saw Zorro darting to the Caplans' front yard. I felt so bad. The cats weren't moving. Had I sacrificed my pet for *nothing*?

I dropped to my knees on the carpet. Defeated. Ruined.

I felt like crying, but I forced it back. I couldn't

keep my shoulders from heaving up and down. I buried my face in my hands.

Then I heard a soft padding sound. I lowered my hands. I saw the dead cats sniffing the air, gazing at the open front door.

Sniffing the mouse?

Without warning, they took off.

They darted past me, brushing me as they went by. They didn't make a sound. They stampeded out the open door, picking up speed as they ran after the mouse.

Bella leaped off Mr. Caplan's lap. The Caplans both uttered startled cries as the black cat hurtled across the carpet and out the front door.

None of us spoke.

We froze there in the living room. The four of us. No cats.

A few seconds later, I heard the squeal of skidding truck tires and Bella's screech of death.

# 35

We stayed silent for a long moment. The silence rang in my ears.

Mr. Caplan jumped up from the couch. His face was very red. A smile spread slowly across it. He slapped me a high five. "Brilliant!" he boomed.

Mrs. Caplan was smiling, too. She stood up and came over to Amanda and me. "Mickey, that was genius," she said. "We couldn't return the dead cats to Cat Heaven. But they could return *themselves*."

"They all ran out to recreate their violent deaths," Mr. Caplan said. "They will be back in Cat Heaven in no time."

Mrs. Caplan let out a long sigh. "Thank goodness that's over," she told her husband. "Let's unpack our bags and then go to Cat Heaven and pick up Bella from the back room. She hates it when we leave her there too long."

Well, I guess it was kind of a happy ending. The Caplans paid Amanda and me an extra fifty dollars each since we had so much trouble.

A few days later, Mom was driving me to my tennis lesson. I'm not a great tennis player. But I'm getting better.

The tennis courts are inside a huge white bubble on the outskirts of town. There are maybe a hundred courts. The smack of tennis balls is deafening.

We were almost there when I saw a store I'd never seen before. "Hey, Mom—stop," I said. I pointed to the big sign over the door. "Check that out."

The store was called Mouse Heaven.

"I have to go in for a minute," I said. I started to open the car door.

Mom held me back. "Mickey, you'll be late for your lesson."

"I'll just be a minute," I said. "I swear."

I darted into the store. A long, narrow store with two rows of glass cages. The air inside smelled of piney wood shavings.

I moved down the two rows of cages. White mice crawled through their shavings or slept curled up on the cage floors. A few stared out at me, twitching their little noses.

I stopped at the very last cage. I lowered my face to the glass.

"Zorro!" I cried. "*There* you are!"

The little guy stared up at me, twitching his tail.

"Zorro!"

*Should I bring him home?*

# WELCOME BACK TO
# THE HALL OF HORRORS

The fire has gone out. The Unliving Room has grown cold. Through the black window I can hear the flap of bat wings as they circle the Tower of No Return.

Did you know the stairs in the Tower only lead UP? They do not lead DOWN.

Don't be tense, Mickey. You will not be staying there. Tonight you will sleep in the guest deadroom.

My assistant is digging your bed right now. The soil will be a soft, welcoming mattress. The tombstone at its head reads: DO NOT DISTURB. So you will have a peaceful sleep.

I am the Story-Keeper, and I will keep your story here in the Hall of Horrors, where it belongs. Tomorrow before you leave, I will have a gift for you. Maybe you can guess what it is.

One word of warning: Don't look in the carrying case till you get home. Shredder gets upset if you look at him. Why is he called Shredder?

Hahahahahahahahaha! Funny question.

Oh, I'm being rude. We have a new guest.

Come right in, young man. I believe your name is Steven Sweeney. Yes?

And you have a story you'd like to tell. It's called *Night of the Giant Everything*. And you think it's scary enough for the Hall of Horrors?

Well, come in, Steven. Just step over that giant python throw pillow. I believe it's napping.

Come in. Plenty of room in the Hall of Horrors. You know. . . . There's Always Room for One More Scream.

# Ready for More?

Here's another tale from the Hall of Horrors:

# NIGHT OF THE
# GIANT EVERYTHING

# 1

"Pick a card. Any card."

I held the deck up to Ava and Courtney. They're in my class. Ava Munroe and Courtney Jackson.

They both laughed. "Steven, we know this trick," Ava said.

Ava is the tallest girl in the sixth grade at Everest Middle School. She's very pretty, with wavy blond hair and blue eyes. But I think being so tall gives her an attitude.

She likes to look down on me. And I'm only two or three inches shorter than she is.

I waved the deck of cards in their faces. "Maybe this trick is different. Go ahead. Pick one and don't tell me what it is."

Courtney crossed her arms in front of her blue hoodie. "It's the ace of hearts," she said without picking a card.

Courtney is black, with short hair and big dark brown eyes. She wears long, dangling earrings and lots of beads. She has a great laugh.

I hear her laugh a lot. Because she likes to laugh at me and my magic tricks.

"How do you know your card will be the ace of hearts?" I asked.

"Because every card in the deck is the ace of hearts," Courtney replied.

She and Ava bumped knuckles and laughed again.

"Okay, okay," I said. "You guessed that one." I tucked the trick deck of cards into my jacket pocket. "But here's a trick you don't know. Can you spare any change?"

I reached up and pulled a quarter from Ava's nose.

Ava groaned. "Steven, that's totally obnoxious. Why are you always doing that?"

*Obnoxious* is one of her favorite words. Her brother is obnoxious. Her dog is obnoxious. Today she said her *lunch* was obnoxious. I'm not kidding.

"I just feel a change in the air," I said. I pulled a quarter from Courtney's ear. I spun it in my fingers and made it disappear.

"Know where the quarter went?" I asked. "Ava, open your mouth."

"No way," she said, spinning away from me.

"Steven, give us a break," Courtney said. "We've seen all your tricks—remember?"

It was a cool fall day. A gust of wind blew my hair over my eyes. I have long, straight black hair. My mom calls it a mop of hair. She likes to wait till I brush it just right and then mess it up with both hands.

Everyone in my family is funny.

Most of the guys in my class have very short hair. But I like it long. It's more dramatic when I'm doing my comedy magic act onstage.

Ava, Courtney, and I were standing at the curb on Everest Street. School had just let out. Kids were still hurrying out of the building. The wind swirled, sending brown leaves dancing down the street.

Courtney tucked her hands into her hoodie. "So tomorrow is the talent assembly?"

I nodded. "Yeah. My act is going to *kill*."

"Not if Courtney and I kill you first!" Ava said.

Ha-ha. LOL. They're both crazy about me. Otherwise, they wouldn't say things like that — right?

"You're my assistants tomorrow," I said. "We have to rehearse the act. Practice your moves."

Courtney squinted at me. "You're not going to pull quarters out of our noses in front of the whole school, are you?"

"Do you have any tricks that aren't obnoxious?" Ava asked.

"For sure," I said. "Here. Check out this new trick."

They didn't see the spray can of Silly String hidden at my side.

I leaned forward. Then I pretended to sneeze on Ava. A biiig sneeze.

And as I sneezed, I squirted a stream of white silly string all over the front of her sweater.

She gasped and staggered back in surprise.

It was a riot.

But then Courtney tried to grab the Silly String can from my hand.

And that's when things went out of control.

Courtney swiped at the can. My finger pushed down on the button. And squirted the stuff all over her face and in her hair.

"Yuck!" She let out a cry and tried to wipe the Silly String gunk from her eyes.

Then Ava grabbed the can and sprayed it on me. I couldn't squirm away. She kept her finger down on the top and covered me in a ton of the sticky stuff. Then she tossed the can to the curb.

I started slapping at the stuff. Trying to pull it off my jacket. Courtney was still rubbing her eyes, smearing it off her cheeks. A big gob was stuck to her hair.

"Steven, do you know how to spell *revenge*?" she asked through gritted teeth.

"Do you know how to spell *joke*?" I shot back.

Kids were laughing and cheering. One kid from the third grade picked up the can from the ground and tried to squirt his friend. But the can was empty.

"Steven, you creep. You ruined my sweater!" Ava cried.

"It comes out," I said. "The can says it's washable. It was just a joke, Ava."

"*You're* a joke!" she cried angrily. She tried to punch me in the gut, but I danced away. I'm smaller and faster.

I glanced at my phone and saw the time. "I'm late for my piano lesson," I said.

I started across the street. But then I turned back and called to Ava. "I'll come to your house after my lesson, and the three of us can rehearse the magic act."

"Not if I see you first!" she shouted.

Courtney waved both fists at me.

I told you. They're crazy about me.

Mr. Pinker is my new piano teacher. He gives lessons from his house, which is just two blocks from the school.

He has a big redbrick house that sits on top of a wide grassy yard that tilts sharply downhill. In the winter, he lets the neighborhood kids use the hill for sledding.

The house is old, with ivy crawling down one wall. It has two chimneys and a long screened-in porch.

I climbed the hill to his house. Rang the bell and let myself in the front door.

The front hall was brightly lit, cluttered with coats and caps and umbrellas hanging on hooks. I could hear piano music from the front room. Someone was finishing a lesson. The house smelled of fresh-baked cookies.

I set down my backpack and tossed my jacket onto one of the hooks. A short red-haired girl gave me a smile as she headed out the front door.

"Hello, Steven. Come in," Mr. Pinker greeted me. "That was Lisa. She got the piano keys all warmed up for you."

He seems like a nice guy. I guess he's about forty or so. He's tall and thin. Mostly bald, with a fringe of red-brown hair around his head. He wears glasses low on his nose.

He always wears a gray suit and a red necktie. This is only my third lesson with him. He's worn the same outfit each time.

I followed him into the front room. It was kind of old-fashioned. Lots of old chairs and a big brown leather couch with the leather peeling off in places. A tall grandfather clock on the far wall had the minute hand missing. It didn't work.

Four black-and-white photographs of sail-boats hung on one wall. A painting of a symphony conductor with his baton raised stood over the mantel.

A low desk in one corner had stacks and stacks of sheet music on it. The piano stood against the other wall, facing the front window. A window seat also held tall stacks of piano sheet music.

Outside, the gusting wind sent a tree branch tapping the front window. It sounded like drumbeats.

"What's that white stuff in your hair?" Mr. Pinker asked. "Are you getting dandruff?"

I reached up. My hair was sticky. "It's Silly String," I said. "I had a little Silly String battle."

He nodded. "Make sure your fingers aren't sticky." Then he disappeared from the room.

A few seconds later, he returned with a big home-baked chocolate chip cookie on a plate and a glass of milk. "I know sixth-graders are hungry after school," he said. "That's why I bake my special cookies for my students every day."

He handed me the plate and set the glass of milk down on a coaster on the piano. I wasn't really hungry, but I didn't want to be rude. I took a big bite of the cookie.

It was very chewy and a gob of it stuck to the roof of my mouth. I tried to wash it down with a sip of milk.

Mr. Pinker pushed the plate under my nose. "Go ahead. Finish it, Steven. All the kids enjoy them."

I forced the cookie down, sipping milk after every bite.

As Mr. Pinker watched me eat, he got this big smile on his face. His eyes lit up and he kept grinning. He watched till I finished every last crumb.

But there was nothing *strange* about that — right?

## About the Author

R.L. Stine's books are read all over the world. So far, his books have sold more than 300 million copies, making him one of the most popular children's authors in history. Besides Goosebumps, R.L. Stine has written the teen series Fear Street and the funny series Rotten School, as well as the Mostly Ghostly series, The Nightmare Room series, and the two-book thriller *Dangerous Girls*. R.L. Stine lives in New York with his wife, Jane, and Minnie, his King Charles spaniel. You can learn more about him at www.RLStine.com.

# DOUBLE THE FRIGHT ALL AT ONE SITE

## www.scholastic.com/goosebumps

### FIENDS OF GOOSEBUMPS & GOOSEBUMPS HORRORLAND CAN:

- PLAY GHOULISH GAMES!
- CHAT WITH FELLOW FAN-ATICS!
- WATCH CLIPS FROM SPINE-TINGLING DVDs!
- EXPLORE CLASSIC BOOKS AND NEW TERROR-IFIC TITLES!
- CHECK OUT THE GOOSEBUMPS HORRORLAND VIDEO GAME!
- GET GOOSEBUMPS PHOTOSHOCK FOR THE IPHONE™ OR IPOD TOUCH®!

◼ SCHOLASTIC

GBWEB

REVENGE OF THE LIVING DUMMY
R.L. STINE

CREEP FROM THE DEEP
R.L. STINE

MONSTER BLOOD FOR BREAKFAST!
R.L. STINE

THE SCREAM OF THE HAUNTED MASK
R.L. STINE

DR. MANIAC VS. ROBBY SCHWARTZ
R.L. STINE

WHO'S YOUR MUMMY?
R.L. STINE

MY FRIENDS CALL ME MONSTER
R.L. STINE

SAY CHEESE – AND DIE SCREAMING!
R.L. STINE

WELCOME TO CAMP SLITHER
R.L. STINE

## 📖 SCHOLASTIC

**www.EnterHorrorLand.com**

GBHL19B

# THE SCARIEST PLACE ON EARTH!

HELP! WE HAVE STRANGE POWERS!
R.L. STINE

ESCAPE FROM HORRORLAND
R.L. STINE

THE STREETS OF PANIC PARK
R.L. STINE

WHEN THE GHOST DOG HOWLS
R.L. STINE

LITTLE SHOP OF HAMSTERS
R.L. STINE

HEADS, YOU LOSE!
R.L. STINE

WEIRDO HALLOWEEN
R.L. STINE

THE WIZARD OF OOZE
R.L. STINE

SLAPPY NEW YEAR!
R.L. STINE

THE HORROR AT CHILLER HOUSE
R.L. STINE

## ■SCHOLASTIC

www.EnterHorrorLand.com

GBHL19B

# The Original Bone-Chilling

## Series

# —with Exclusive Author Interviews!

# R. L. Stine's Fright Fest!

# NEED MORE THRILLS?

## Get Goosebumps!

## PLAY

Wii. PlayStation 2

NINTENDO DS

## WATCH

## LISTEN

■SCHOLASTIC

www.scholastic.com/goosebumps